IRISH CASTLE MURDER

A CASTLE TOURS OF IRELAND COZY MYSTERY BOOK 1

PENNY BROOKE

CHAPTER ONE

*A*ll around me, people were already on the move. As soon as the plane touched down on the runway, I heard the familiar click of seatbelts being loosened and almost immediately, the aisle filled up with happy travelers anxious to escape the claustrophobic environment that had confined them for more than ten hours.

As for me, I gazed out the window, content to wait until the aisles were clear and there was little hassle in retrieving my carry-on bag from the overhead compartment. I heard the rise and fall of laughter all around me, but I was barely conscious of it. My mind was elsewhere, deep in thought as I took in the lush green surroundings of what I considered absolute heaven on earth.

It always felt good to know that my feet were once again firmly planted on the ground. The climb up through the obscure haze of cumulus clouds is exciting for most people, but for some reason, I have never been a part of that crowd. I always suck in a deep breath at take-off, and usually, I won't give another complete exhale until I feel the wheels of the plane touch down again when I know I'm safely on the ground. That's where I know I should be. Sure, flying is safe, and I have little or nothing to worry about. Still, I feel the only natural thing I can rely on is the ground underneath my feet.

My eyes drifted upward to the brightness of the sky, and a faint smile graced the corners of my mouth. Nothing like taking in the beautiful azure blue of the Irish sky. It wasn't just the color that struck me but also the warm, nostalgic feeling that came with it. There's something ethereal and soft about the Irish landscape, especially in springtime.

Then my mind drifted to Grams' old house. The place we often visited as kids. It had always been my second home. I can remember so well my brother playing on the lawns of Gladstone Castle in Cable Creek with me. Those memories could be compared to no other place on earth, and I felt my heart skip a beat in anticipation of seeing its grand towers once again.

Situated high up on top of a hill, our family home was indeed a sight to behold. It seemed to grow right up out of the landscape, seemingly defying nature. How many years had it stood there? I knew that if I asked my grams, she'd instantly recall and relate every detail of its history without hesitation.

I couldn't remember the last time I felt so relaxed. And why not? I was back in my favorite place in the whole world. I waited patiently while all the other passengers crowded the aisles waiting for the doors to open so they could escape from the tin can they'd been stuck in. A flash of irritation flooded over me—I knew they weren't going to get out quickly. They never did, and it baffled me that they'd continue to try.

When the doors finally opened, I watched impatiently as the other passengers pushed their way out of the cabin. Happy to be able to stretch their legs and feel a taste of freedom once again. I finally had enough space to maneuver my large bag from the overhead bin without worrying about bumping into anyone. The bag was heavy, and I had stuffed it so full that it didn't want to budge.

By the time I managed to wrest it free, I was practically the only person left on the plane. The aisle was clear, and I could walk right through the gate into the belly of Dublin's *Aerfort Bhaile Átha Cliath*.

It was easy to make my way now. I'd taken this walk so often that I didn't even need to look for directions. Leaving Terminal 2, I knew exactly where to find the luggage carousel, but that wasn't where I was headed. I had packed sparsely with only my overhead bag to see me through the first few days. Packing anything I couldn't do without—and nothing more—would save me time from checking bags and waiting in the crowd for my luggage to come down the slide. That way, I could avoid fighting against the crowd just to retrieve it. As for me...I planned to go shopping the first chance I got. If I had my way, it would be the first thing tomorrow morning.

Following the signs to immigration, I was anxious to get through the rigamarole. Border agents always made me feel a little nervous.

Even though I was one of the last to leave the plane, I was the first to go through immigration. I handed my passport and documents to the customs agent, and he barely gave me a glance. Had he been trained to not smile? Opening my passport, he raised his eyes only once and gave me a cursory glance. Then he ran my passport through the reader and waited.

"Annabelle Shannon?" he asked, sounding incredibly bored.

"Yes."

"How long will you be staying in Ireland?"

I hesitated to answer. I didn't know how long I would stay. "I'm not sure," I said honestly. "But at least a few weeks."

He didn't say anything. "What is the purpose of your visit?"

"I'm visiting my grandmother."

I thought I saw a flicker of approval in his eyes, but I couldn't be sure.

"Where will you be staying?"

"Cable Creek."

His hands froze for just a fraction of a beat before he turned his attention back to his job.

"Do you know it?" I dared to ask.

"No, but I've heard of it." He stamped my book, closed it with a snap, and handed it back to me. "Welcome to Ireland. Enjoy your stay."

Before I could respond, he was already beckoning for the next person in line. I quickly gathered my things and passed through the doors that led out into the main lobby, where crowds of people had gathered to collect their family, friends, business partners, and other assorted travelers.

Having made this trip so many times, I would normally have had the whole thing down to a science. Of course, it helped to have my grams here to make sure my comfort level was well taken care of. I knew that I would have the best of everything when it came to good meals, a soft bed to sleep in, and a home base to operate from.

The noise of the crowd outside caught me off guard. I had been deep in my own thoughts, and it brought me full awake in an instant. I had reserved a rental car when I'd purchased my tickets, but Grams had insisted that I cancel it.

"Belle," she had said. "There is no reason to spend your money on a car when I have a perfectly good one right here. I'll ask Spencer to pick you up at the airport, and you can have my car while you're here." It didn't matter how much I insisted; she would have it no other way.

My eyes scanned the crowd for Spencer, but I could barely remember what he looked like. It had been several years since I'd been here, and he was scarcely a part of my memory. I just remembered this awkward, skinny guy who lived down the road a short distance from Grams. I sighed a little and brushed a strand of hair away from my face, trying to see if there were any familiar faces in the crowd, but honestly, I didn't know what I was looking for.

I didn't see him at first, but there was no mistaking the sound of my name from a voice that was more than a few decibels above the crowd. Embarrassed, I turned toward the sound and saw him standing there. He was much taller than I had remembered, with long, lanky legs. He still had a pockmarked face that made you think he had never gotten past his teenage acne phase but looked much older. He was waving his arms frantically to get my attention. Feeling the rush of embarrassment flood my cheeks, I looked around to see if anyone else had noticed, but the crowd was not focused on Spencer or me. They were still searching the collection of faces for their own guests.

I hurriedly pushed my way through them all until I reached him, knowing that would be the only way to silence him from constantly shouting out my name. For a minute, I just stood there, not sure what the proper protocol was for greeting your grams' neighbor. I felt just a tad bit relieved when he bent down and gave me a perfunctory hug before reaching for my bag.

"Is this all you have, Belle?" he asked as he pointed me in the direction he wanted me to go.

"Yep. That's it."

"Man, you travel light."

"Not usually, but I planned this trip kind of on the spur of the moment. I didn't have much time to prepare." I didn't want to tell him all my personal details.

I wasn't sure how much to even tell Grams or whether I wanted him to know. After all, he was just the neighbor.

"How was your flight?" he asked, more as a means to fill the awkward silence that fell between us than out of genuine interest.

"Pretty good. At least as far as flights go. I slept most of the way, caught up on some reading, that sort of stuff."

"Well, it's good that you're here. I know your grams was really happy when she found out you were coming."

"I really miss her. I wish we could get her to come to the States. I would guess she's pretty lonely here by herself."

We were in the parking lot now. He pointed me in the direction of the car and clicked the key fob to open the door, and at the same time, tossed my bag into the back seat like it weighed no more than a feather. Within minutes, we were on the highway heading north into the lush green hills of Ireland.

Far from the drab buildings and variations of brown hues of New York, it took a minute for my eyes to adjust to all the colors that surrounded me. It always boggled my mind to hear people talk of how beautiful the city was when someplace like Ireland barely got noticed.

It had been several years since I'd been here, and while I knew it would happen, I was surprised to see that some things had changed. What was once an open field where children used to play had now become a shopping center or business community. It made me a little sad to see so much of the natural beauty of the Irish landscape disappearing so quickly.

Soon, we were leaving the city proper behind and on the open road. My mind kept jumping back to my last day at the office and my excitement at seeing Grams for the first time in years. That day had given me a good reason to pause.

First, Grams' phone call seemed very strange. I knew she had been getting up in years, but our last conversation had caused me alarm. She said nothing specific, but we had talked frequently over the years, so I knew by the tone of her voice that she was holding something back. Her voice had sounded tired and weak like maybe she had been sick. When I'd asked her about it, she avoided the subject by telling me all about the new Hardcastle Hotel that was soon to open. As one of the local tour guides in the community, she had been invited to be one of the first guests to spend the night there. She was excited but didn't want to go alone and called to ask me to accompany her.

Since I was never one to turn down an opportunity to visit this glorious place, it took less than a minute for me to agree. Partly because I felt it had been too long since I'd been here, and partly because I wanted to see for myself that Grams was the same loving person I remembered.

She wasn't old per se, but I knew she was getting along in years, and living here all alone couldn't be good for her. The rest of the family had all moved to the States years before, leaving her here all by herself. No matter how much we pleaded, she had dug in her heels and refused to leave her homeland. No amount of pleading or coercion would move her to change her mind. I didn't like that she was so far away, but I knew there was no convincing her, and now that I was back on these glorious roads and my eyes were soaking in the landscape, I had to say that I couldn't blame her.

"So, Spencer," I started tentatively. "How is Grams doing? Is she okay here by herself?"

He let out a long exhale that sounded like he was letting the air out of a balloon.

"She's fine…she's fine," he said quietly. I thought I heard a note of concern in his voice.

"Really?"

"Well, of course, she could be better. I know your grams has a lot of energy for a woman her age, but it can't be good for her to spend all her time up on that hill all alone."

"I know what you mean," I agreed. "We have been

trying to convince her to leave for years, but she won't budge."

"I guess it's hard for us to understand her connection to the land."

"Oh, I think I understand it. I feel it too when I'm here. It's just that I'm not sure it's practical for her to continue trying to do everything by herself. I worry about her too, you know. What if something happened to her and she's there rambling around in that big old place all alone. Who would know?"

"Charlotte and I, we both come down and check on her almost every day, but I do think she should consider having someone move in with her so she could have some company. We can't always be there."

"I know, I know," I told him. "I'm going to try to have another heart to heart with her while I'm here."

"That would be so good, Belle. By the way, how long are you staying this time?"

"Not sure. I took a leave from work, so I can stay longer than the usual two weeks."

"That's great! I know she's going to love that."

It was hard to suppress a smile as we turned off the main highway and were now careening through the rolling hills all around. The sights and sounds of the city had long ago faded into the background, and I could feel the tension of city life already slipping away. I had to admit, I needed this break more than anything else, probably more than my grams. My life as a lawyer was beginning to take its toll. I spent most of my waking hours preparing briefs and making court appearances, and the little time I once had for life's little pleasures had long ago gone up in smoke. It had been working, eating, sleeping, and back to work again for longer than I cared to admit.

Spencer turned off the radio, rolled down the window, and immediately all that is Ireland floated in. I took in a deep breath and tasted the salt in the sea air on my tongue mixed with the aroma of fresh grass from the surrounding meadows.

We slowed down to nearly a crawl as we came upon an old tractor bumbling slowly down the road. Suddenly, a new smell entered the car, one that I had forgotten was also a part of the Irish landscape. The tractor's cargo had an unmistakable odor, and no doubt, it was on its way to deliver a supply of fresh fertilizer to one of the nearby farms.

We quickly rolled the windows back up and had a good laugh about it as we tried to wait patiently until there was a chance to pass the tractor or it would turn off one of the side roads. Happily, it didn't take too long before it turned down a crumbly dirt road and out of reach of my senses.

I chuckled. "I forgot about that part of Ireland."

"Yeah, I would forget about it too if I could," Spencer agreed.

Taking note of the familiar surroundings, I realized we were only a few kilometers from my grams' place. My heart skipped a beat, and my eagerness to see her in the flesh was difficult to control. I couldn't wait. It had been too long since my last visit.

CHAPTER TWO

he familiar sight of the Cable Creek sign told me we had only a little way to go. The long, windy road made it impossible to hurry, so we slowed down and took in the view. Overhead, the sky was almost entirely free of clouds, a rarity for this part of the world. I had to blink a few times after being momentarily blinded by its brightness.

In the distance, I could see my destination perched on top of a hill just a few short kilometers away. The massive stone structure looked like part of the landscape as if it had been there all along. It might as well have been; the house had been in our family for who knows how many generations. It was the one thing I was always proud to boast about in America. No matter how much my friends bragged about their fancy homes, none of them could ever hold a candle to my photographs of a genuine family castle. Americans just couldn't do that.

Spencer slowed down even more so he wouldn't miss the small one-lane road that led up the hill. The surrounding ivy had grown so dense that the entryway was almost completely covered. My first thought was why Grams had let it get that way. She was always a stickler for perfection, and again my thoughts drifted to the possibility that things were not as good as she had always claimed.

The car climbed the hill slowly. The path was well worn, but the cobblestone drive was no match for the relentless tendrils of grass and the spread of the moss that now forced its way up through the cracks to reclaim space on the hillside.

Before long, we pulled up in front of the grand entryway. "Impressive" was the only word I could think of as I stared at the massive front doors ideally situated at the top of an elegant set of steps. A smile formed on my face at the sight.

"It's good to be home again," I breathed out loud. I blinked a few times, startled when the large doors burst open and a young girl about twelve years old came skipping out. It took a few seconds to recognize her as Spencer's younger sister. I scrunched up my brow, searching the recesses of my mind to recall her name.

Oh, Charlotte, that's it. It had been a long time, and she looked much more mature now. No more of those childlike freckles sprayed across her face, and the little-girl pigtails had now been combed back into a single French braid that ran down her back.

She ran to the car with the kind of glee that only someone her age could have. She was still a little bit girl-ish, but evidence of a little lady was slowly beginning to emerge. Before I could get out and come to a complete stand, she had wrapped her arms around me and squeezed as hard as she could. These were times when I really hated myself. I just wasn't that much into people, especially kids. Still, this one obviously intended to attach herself to me regardless of what I thought.

Reluctantly, I returned the embrace and looked up. It didn't matter much anyway; the sight I had been longing to see since I'd decided to come here was waiting. My grams was standing there at the top of the steps, her arms outstretched and eager to embrace me. She looked a little too thin for my taste, and the signs of all her ups and downs were clearly etched in lines all over her face, but there was no mistaking that bright smile and kind, loving eyes. She had gone through all the phases of life: a young, vibrant girl full of vim and vigor, a middle-aged businesswoman, and now a mature woman entering her senior years. My heart filled with pride and love at the sight of her, and a warm glow spread right through me.

I wanted to rush up and hold her in my arms, but young Charlotte had yet to release her grip on me. What had I done to deserve this kind of affection?

Finally, I was able to loosen her grip long enough so I could start up the steps, but Charlotte was more tenacious than I would have imagined. She wrapped her long arms around my waist again and climbed the stairs with me, matching my every step. She had already started an incessant chatter that I was barely hearing.

Grams stood erect as an arrow and watched our interaction with a hint of humor in her eyes. She knew all too well how I was around children, and it amused her to no end to see one so happy to be in my company.

I smiled back at her, understanding her amusement. We were like that. Out of all the others in the family, we were the only ones who were totally in sync. I could always tell what she was thinking, and she knew me all too well.

I reached the top of the steps and couldn't wait to wrap my arms around her. Alarm bells rang in my head as I pulled her in close. She was even thinner than before, and I could feel her tiny bones poking through the skin.

"Grams, is everything all right?"

"Yes, dear. Everything is just fine," she said as she held my hands in hers, gripping them tightly with surprising strength.

I wrapped my arm around her waist, and we walked inside together. The castle was even better than I remembered. The exterior wall gave no hint to the grandeur found inside. We entered the main foyer, where we dispensed with our coats and outdoor attire. Grams had been wearing a bulky sweater, and when she took it off, I could see how just the last few years since we were together had taken their toll. I couldn't wait to have an honest sit-down with her so we could talk it out, but she was having none of that today.

"Charlotte, why don't you let Annabelle catch her wind now? Go on upstairs and find Peggy so we can give her a little time to settle in."

"Yes, ma'am," the girl said and immediately disappeared through the main door and up the grand staircase.

I could feel the tension leaving my shoulders as I watched her walk away.

"What shall I do with her bag?" Spencer asked.

"You can take it upstairs to her room, Spencer. Thank you," she told him. Then she turned all her attention on me, studying me with those piercing blue eyes that seemed to reach right down into my soul. "Now that that's settled," she continued as she linked her arm in mine again. "Why don't you take a load off and join me in a cup of afternoon tea?"

There was no resistance on my part. I was more than happy for her to lead me through these familiar hallways. We didn't go into the great room, her usual custom. Instead, she led me down the darkened hall and into a small anteroom near the kitchen. There she had a cozy little setup. In one corner was a large window with a view of the gardens. Through the open windows, the soft aroma of flowers wafted in. The warm glow from the fireplace made it the perfect place to catch up, and I didn't regret missing out on tea in the massive great room at all. I had plenty of time to see the rest of the place later.

"Why are we back here?" I asked. I had barely had a glimpse of the rest of the home as we passed through. I sat properly like she'd taught me with my fingers clasped together in my lap and my legs crossed at the ankles and gazed out the two arched windows on either side of the chimney. She excused herself and disappeared into the kitchen to prepare the tea. She seemed happy enough, but I was still concerned.

I heard her voice coming from the kitchen. "Well," she started. "I decided that it was only me in this big old place. I didn't see much reason for using the whole house. I can live quite comfortably in this room and kitchen. It's just too much for me to maintain."

I walked to the door, so I could watch her as she prepared the tea. "Can I help?" I asked.

"Oh don't be silly, child," she said with a cluck of her tongue. "I have been preparing tea since I was knee-high to a grasshopper. I can do this blindfolded."

I knew better than to argue about it. Grams was just as stubborn as I was, and I knew I would lose. I sighed and turned around to examine the room she had left me in. It was tidy enough, but I could see a layer of dust on the surface of the table. I could tell she had been trying to tidy up a bit on her own, but it seemed like she was fighting a losing battle. No doubt, her age was beginning to get to her.

"Is Margaret still working for you?"

"Oh yes, she is but not as much as she used to. She only comes and helps me once a week. The rest of the time, it's just me here alone. That's why I moved down here. It's just too much work for me to maintain by myself, and I don't really trust anyone new to come in here and take care of the house for me."

I nodded my head to show I understood and went back to my seat to wait.

"Tomorrow, dear, I'll show you around so you can see what's been happening here in town. You'll be so surprised." She appeared at the door with a silver tray spread with all of my favorites. Of course, she always served that Irish breakfast tea that I loved so well, but she also had an entire tray of croissants, jams, jellies, and other flavorful things.

"Grams!" I exclaimed. "How are we going to eat all of this?"

She set the tray down on the table and patted me on my knee, smiling. "One bite at a time. One bite at a time."

I couldn't wait to dig in, but I asked more questions. "Grams, are you sure you're all right?" I asked again.

"I'm fine."

I gave her a scrutinizing look. "You don't look so good. You're even thinner than you used to be, and you seem to be having some…financial problems."

"Financial problems? What do you mean?"

"Well, the drive up is all overgrown. It doesn't look like it's been cleared in more than a year. The house is dark, and you've moved into this tiny little space. I can't help but wonder if this is because of money issues."

She let out a soft chuckle as she started pouring the tea. "Don't be silly. I'm healthy enough to eat flies." She laughed. "As for finances, it's all good. Since I'm not using this big old castle anymore, I figured I could put my money to better use than in this money pit. For now, everything is going into the bank."

"And what would you like to do with it?" I asked.

"I'm thinking of doing a bit of traveling."

I was surprised. "Grams, you have never wanted to leave Ireland. Ever. How many times have we asked you to come for a visit and you refused?"

"I know. I've been a stubborn old mule about that; I admit it. But I miss having family around. I love the history of this place. The romance of the hills and the wonders of the castle life, but it's not enough for me anymore. I need to be around people, so I don't turn into a grumpy old hermit." She passed me a cup of tea and a plate to serve myself from all the treats she had laid out for us. "Don't get me wrong. I love it here in my castle. I wouldn't give it up for the world. But, I think that now that the family is gone and is showing no desire to return except for an occasional visit, I'm happy to see other parts of the world, too."

I nodded my head in understanding, relieved that she was not planning on leaving Ireland for good.

"I'm retiring next year, and I'll have a lot of free time on my hands."

"Retiring?!" My second time to be shocked.

She gave me a soft smile, and there was that twinkle in her eye again.

"What are you up to, Grams?"

"Yes, I'm retiring. I'm getting too old to do all the walking required for my work. Taking people on castle tours is still fun, but my legs don't carry me like they used to. I get tired quickly, and I just can't keep up. I want to do something different before I lose their use altogether."

"Are you sick?"

"Of course not. I've been to my doctor, and he says I'm perfectly fine for someone my age. I still have a lot of energy, but I just want to use it for something different." She set her cup down and folded her hands in her lap. "That's why I called you," she said with a sudden look of seriousness on her face.

I let my eyes meet hers. "Yes, you were very mysterious on the phone."

"I know. I didn't mean to be. I knew that out of all my grandchildren, you would be the one to come through for me." She paused, and I could feel her watching me closely. "I know how much you love your life in New York City, and I admire you for it. But I was hoping I could convince you to spend more time here in Cable Creek."

"And do what?" I asked, eyebrows raised.

"Help me, here. I know you won't make the big bucks

you're used to getting in that fancy city life you lead, but here you won't need it."

I was too stunned to speak.

"Tell me about New York, work, the family, everything. I want to hear it all," she continued.

I gave a dismissive wave of my hand. "We've got plenty of time for that, Grams. I'll be here for a while."

"Really?" She raised a suspicious eyebrow as she glanced in my direction. "What about your job? You always told me that your job was so important you couldn't leave it for too long."

I hunched my shoulders like a schoolgirl, afraid to say too much. I didn't know how to tell her that I needed a break, and I wasn't even sure if I wanted to go back.

"Well, things have changed a bit now," I said. "I am free to take a little more time off these days."

"It's too much for you, huh?"

Somehow I wasn't surprised at her question. She always knew what I was thinking, no matter how much I tried to hide it.

"You may think I don't know how you feel, dear, but I do."

I smiled inwardly; it was hard not to. The two of us were always in sync, and she always knew what I was thinking even before I did.

"You don't have to answer me right now," she continued, "but I'd hope that you would at least take some time to think about it. You can even have my job since I'll be retiring soon."

"Me? A tour guide? That's something I hadn't thought of."

"Sure, why not?"

"You know me, Grams. I'm not as social as you. Chatting up a bunch of strangers about history just isn't really my cup of tea."

"I know, I know. If you're not debating a difficult court case or involved in some hard-nosed business negotiations, you feel lost. But I can assure you that being a tour guide can be just as challenging."

I sat back in my chair and let out a long breath. I wasn't about to debate the issue. I would never win, and I knew that going in. So, I just agreed to think about it, and we moved on to discuss new subjects.

The door opened, and Peggy came in with Charlotte following closely behind.

"Excuse me, Mrs. Gladstone. Sorry to interrupt."

"Yes?"

"We're done for now. I'm going to take Charlotte home. Is there anything else you need before I go?"

"Take Charlotte home? Why? Where's Spencer?"

"He left to help his dad."

"Hmm." Grams absentmindedly looked at the large grandfather clock in the corner. "I hadn't realized how late it was. Thank you so much, Peggy. I'm fine for now. I'll see you next week."

I stared at the woman quizzically.

"Oh, I'm so sorry. I didn't introduce you," Grams said. "Annabelle, this is Peggy—Spencer and Charlotte's mother. She's been helping me do a little bit of work around here. Peggy, this is my granddaughter, Annabelle."

We exchanged greetings, and they left. I was surprised to see that the sun had already set as Grams walked with me up the back staircase to what was to be my room. It was spacious accommodations, and now I understood what Peggy had been doing all this time— putting the finishing touches on what Grams was hoping would be my new living quarters. The room was large enough to put my entire New York apartment inside and still have room to spare. There was a soft yellow glow from the large fireplace across from the bed, making it nice and warm and cozy, a welcome feeling I had missed from the nippy winters in the city. It was evident that the old furniture I remembered was gone and replaced with a large canopy bed, fully decked out with curtains drawn all around. There were more pillows than I could count on the bed, each with its own frilly fringes and the soft scent of potpourri in the air.

"Grams, when did you do all of this?"

"Oh, I didn't do it. This is all Peggy's doing. You know I don't have a decorator's bone in my body. She's a fine room designer, so I charged her with making a place that would help you feel more at home."

I looked around the room and smiled. "Well, she did a wonderful job. I love it. I couldn't have asked for anything more."

In fact, I felt so comfortable in this new room that I couldn't wait to crawl in the bed and drift off to sleep. Suddenly, the hours of travel caught up to me. Grams stayed for only a few minutes before she, too, felt the exhaustion of such a busy day and left me alone. It took only minutes before I was neatly under the covers and drifting off to sleep.

The next morning, I was awakened by a rush of noises floating up the stairs from down below. I don't know how long the chatter had been going on as I was deep in slumber. The time difference and the exhaustion from the long flight had finally taken their toll. It took a few minutes to realize that something didn't sound quite right. With just me and Grams here, the house should've been quiet, but there was just too much noise wafting up from the floor below. My mind began to race with all sorts of horrific possibilities. My heart felt like it had come to a complete stop as I thought about what could have happened.

There should have only been the two of us in the house. Still, I could clearly hear several different and unfamiliar voices floating through the door, and they all sounded very agitated. What could have happened since we talked last night?

Without a second thought, I jumped out of bed, grabbed my robe, and pulled it on as I ran down the stairs. The toes of my bare feet curled up from contact with the cold stone floor, but I didn't hesitate to slip them into my warm, fuzzy slippers as I bolted out into the hallway and down the stairs.

CHAPTER THREE

"What's wrong? What's...what's going on?" I asked as I burst through the door to my grams' parlor. My panicked entrance was quickly followed by embarrassment when I saw her sitting in her parlor chatting it up with a room full of people I didn't know.

"Oh, Annabelle, you're up. I hope you slept well." Grams gave me a cursory look up and down. "You really shouldn't walk around in your bare feet here. You'll catch your death from the cold."

I nodded as I became painfully aware that I had no idea of the impression my abrupt appearance had made on these people. My first instinct was to run back to my room and hide, but it was too late for that. "What's going on?" I asked instead, trying to pretend I had not just made an embarrassing mistake.

"It's wonderful news," she answered, clasping her hands together. "These people are the ones I told you about from the Hardcastle Hotel." She gestured to two gentlemen sitting directly across from her.

"Oh yeah." I gave a cursory nod to the group before turning my attention back to her.

"It's officially opening next month, and we're going to be staying there tonight." She was so excited about it, she seemed barely able to contain herself.

"Tonight?" I fiddled around with the tie of my robe, hoping for a chance to escape. "That's nice," I mumbled, gazing around at the people in the room. I felt so stupid.

"But, there is a catch," said one man sitting in the corner of the room. "We each have to write a review of the experience and share it with our followers on our respective social media pages."

"That's nice," I mumbled again as I backed out toward the door.

Once I was out the door, I could hear the group all burst back into excited chatter. It was almost impossible to believe, but in their excitement, none of them seemed to notice my unkempt appearance, but I was still completely mortified. As soon as I had escaped the parlor, I fled back to my own room. What was I thinking about running out like that?

Regaining my composure, I pulled out a pair of jeans from my sizable overnight bag. A sudden realization struck me: I desperately needed to go shopping today, especially now that I'd embarrassed myself so completely. I was sure that a new wardrobe would pick up my spirits, but now I wasn't so sure I would have the time. I had thought I would have at least had a few days before visiting the Hardcastle. Still, Grams had already committed us for tonight, and I was sure she had a full schedule already laid out for me to do.

I had hoped we'd be spending some quality time together before this event and didn't expect to be tossed into the fray so quickly. As reluctant as I was to embrace all that is Ireland, I knew that I could not disappoint her. She had been counting on me for so long, and I knew I had to put off whatever I wanted to do until her needs were met, so jeans, for now, was my only option.

We arrived at the Hardcastle early in the afternoon. Grams didn't want to wait until everyone else came; she wanted to have free rein of the place to form her own opinions long before others put their input in.

The place was breathtakingly beautiful. I was impressed even before we arrived at the front entrance. Unlike the broken-down cobblestone drive that led to our family estate, this one was well-manicured and lined with cherry trees, all now in full bloom. Their tiny pink blossoms offered a spray of color that welcomed everyone who came to a warm and inviting place. On either side of the drive was a paved walkway, lined with colorful bushes I couldn't identify, each blooming with every hue you could imagine. My eyes followed the walkway until it led into a crop of trees that stopped just before a lake. I would guess that's where guests could spend their time picnicking, fishing, or some other outdoor activity. The scene was far more than I had imagined, and we hadn't even arrived at the hotel yet.

The car that came to pick us up drove into a circular drive and stopped in front of a grand stairway, which led to a massive entryway. I was proud of my ancestral home, but it was nothing compared to this. When we entered, we found ourselves in an enormous foyer with a beautiful black and white checkered marble floor.

"Grams, look. Check out this floor!"

She gave me a knowing smile. "I know you've probably never seen anything like this in New York, have you?"

"I've seen marble before, but not like this." I stooped down to get a closer look at its design. "It's so unique."

"That's because in the castles here, all the marble is hand-blown."

I followed the floor design from the doorway into a grand room to our left. It was even more impressive with nineteenth-century furnishings, massive tapestries on the walls, and a collection of art pieces that looked to be originals. I'm no art expert, but it was enough to leave me completely awestruck.

From the opposite side of the room I saw a middle-aged man dressed in a vintage nineteenth-century suit, complete with a black coat with tails. He stopped close to where I was examining the detail of the flooring and stooped down beside me. He leaned in close enough so that I could catch a whiff of his cologne.

"You see," he started to explain as he ran his hands along the lines of the marble. "Modern marble is all machine-made, so its design is entirely uniform, but this was all made by hand, so each tile has its own unique look."

"Wow!" was all I could manage to get out as I tried to pull myself back up into a good standing position.

"Welcome!" he said as he stood up and gave us his most dashing smile. I felt like I had slipped back into one of those historical movies. I didn't know who he was, but he was certainly playing his part. He looked like he had just stepped out of a history book with his cravat tied perfectly around his neck, leather shoes, and a kilt. He definitely had the appearance of the real thing.

"Welcome to the new Hardcastle Hotel. My name is Liam, and I'm here to make sure that your every need is met in true Irish fashion."

He went on to explain that the entryway had been there for at least two hundred years and took pains to point out every detail of its design. At the same time, another man came and quickly collected our bags and disappeared through the massive doors with them.

While the castle had been around for nearly eight hundred years, the remodeling was shown to reflect nineteenth-century Ireland, and not all the way back to the Middle Ages. Above the fireplace hung the portrait of the patriarch of the Hardcastle family still looking down on his charges centuries later. The beautiful marble floor had now been dotted in different places with what appeared to be handmade rugs designed to reflect the color of the tapestries and artwork around the room. Over the window, a massive curtain had been pulled back to let in as much natural sunlight as possible.

"Nice to meet you, Liam," I said, feeling like I sounded a little too much like a schoolgirl. He was definitely someone to put in the front to greet the guests. With just a little gray around his temples and his striking good looks, I would guess they'd have the women clientele all sewed up.

"My name is Annabelle," I said, gesturing with my hand on my chest. "And this is my grandmother, Clarissa Gladstone."

"It's nice to see you again, Mrs. Gladstone," he said with a little wink. "And nice to see you again too, Annabelle," he said with a smile.

His words confused me for a second. "We've met before?" I asked.

"Not officially," he replied. "But I still can't get your grand appearance this morning out of my head."

It took only a second before I remembered the embarrassing entrance I had made when I thought Grams was in trouble. "Oh," I said, trying to fight back a blush. "I didn't realize you were there. I'm so sorry about that."

"No worries. We've all had some moments like that. Trust me, no one here is going to hold that against you. If you have any questions or require anything during your stay, please feel free to ask me."

He certainly was the perfect host for this opening. He had only said a few words, but I was already intrigued and wondered what else I would learn on the castle tour. He explained a few details about the castle's history but, to our disappointment, had opted to reserve the remainder of the tour until the rest of the guests arrived.

"Is it okay if we walk around a bit on our own?" Grams asked.

"Yes, of course," he told us. "If you like, we can take you to your room so you can settle in while you wait, but the official tour will start when the entire group has arrived."

CHAPTER FOUR

Our room was equally as grand as the rest of the castle, and I relished in settling in. While Grams and I had to share the room, it was pretty large and more than comfortable. With one bed in one end of the room and the other on the opposite side, it was almost like we were in separate rooms. The middle area had an excellent living section with a television, desk, and vanity. Opposite the vanity was a massive bathroom complete with a huge soaking tub and a built-in sauna. It was the pinnacle of luxury. But it was the bed that pulled me away. We had planned to walk around the grounds and view the gardens, but once I'd lain down in the plush softness, there was little chance that I was going to get up anytime soon. It was only after a soft knock on the door announcing that our presence was needed downstairs that I reluctantly pulled myself away from my own personal cocoon.

We made our way down to the great room, and I paused on the stairs when I saw the crowd. I could already feel the knots tying up my stomach. There were many more people than I had imagined. I had expected there to be only about four or five others there, but clearly, more than twenty guests had all gathered. I groaned inside, already feeling overwhelmed.

"Oh, Annabelle," I heard my name called out from somewhere in the back. I turned my gaze to see Liam beckoning me to join the group. Sucking in my breath, I descended the stairs behind Grams as if I was using her as a human shield. I have no idea why crowds of people made me so nervous. In the courtroom, it was different. I could easily hold my own around so many people because I wasn't expected to talk to most of them. I was so engrossed in the job that nothing could distract me. But here, among all these strangers, it was something different. I would not engage in a business negotiation or a tangible debate, something I could base my responses on. This was all social, and as much as I loved Irish history and culture, I didn't feel at all like I was ready to go toe to toe with some of Ireland's finest.

I studied the crowd as I descended the stairs, already trying to get a bead on each guest. I tried to figure out how many of them had seen me that morning looking so unkempt. I pushed that thought out of my mind because that was really going to mess me up for the night.

Liam cleared his throat. "Before we begin our tour, and since you are all going to be neighbors for the weekend, it would be nice if you all got to know each other. I've arranged for a cozy dinner in the dining room so we can all get acquainted. If you could follow me, please."

I barely heard a word he was saying as we entered the dining hall. Grams and I sat next to each other at the long table. How on earth were we going to get to know each other sitting at such a large table? It was big enough for everyone to have a seat but not close enough to converse comfortably with anyone other than those sitting directly across or next to you.

Grams and I choose seats right in the middle. Right away, I could tell that she knew everyone quite well, whereas I didn't know anyone, no one at all. Across from us sat a somewhat classy dressed woman who introduced herself as she handily reached across the table and grabbed a dinner roll from one of the serving dishes.

"Hi, I'm Georgina," she said, reaching her hand across the table to shake mine. "You must be Annabelle. It's so nice to finally meet you."

I was surprised she already knew who I was. No doubt, it was either Grams had been talking me up, or maybe it was some of her guests that had been in her parlor that morning. I felt a little out of my element. These people already knew enough about me, but I knew nothing about them. I glanced sideways at my grams, who only smiled a little before turning to an elderly couple sitting next to her.

"Hi, Georgina," I said, trying to show more confidence than I felt. "Yes, I'm Annabelle."

"So, you're from New York, I hear. I've always wanted to see New York, but I've only seen it in the movies. It looks so glamorous. Tell me, is it really like that? What do you do there? Have you always lived there? Can I come and visit you sometime?"

She had already settled into an incessant chatter that looked like it was never going to end. She asked question after question but never paused long enough to give me a chance to respond. I was convinced that she only wanted to hear herself speak and was not genuinely interested in hearing what I had to say. I was already trying to find a way to get out of the conversation before it had already started.

Grams seemed to have found an elderly couple that she knew pretty well to my right. They looked about the same age and quickly struck up a conversation. Grams could see my distress being immediately roped into a conversation with Georgina, so she quickly came to my rescue.

"Georgina," she started. "Can I interrupt you for a moment? I'd like to introduce the O'Brians to my grand-daughter."

Georgina looked like she had been slapped, but she nodded her head in agreement and immediately turned to a woman on her right and began chatting with her. With relief, I turned my attention to Grams so she could introduce us.

"Annabelle, this is Patrick and Lillian O'Brian. They are also long-standing residents of Cable Creek."

"Nice to meet you, Annabelle." They spoke almost in unison.

"Nice to meet you, too," I said, relieved to have someone semi-normal to talk to. "When you say long-standing, how long do you mean?"

"Like your grandmother, our families have lived here for many generations," Mrs. O'Brian said.

"Is that right?" I admired the pride they showed in their heritage. "I'd love to learn a little of your family's history while I'm here."

"Yes, we'd love to share it with you. How long are you planning to stay? We'd love to have you come for a visit before you go. We are also planning to do something with our little place. It won't be as grand as this, but it'll be nice."

"I'd love that."

"Yes, Cable Creek has a very vibrant history, and I'm hoping to get Annabelle to make this an extended stay if I can," Grams interjected. "She's the one I told you about. She's always been interested in the history of Cable Creek and of Ireland itself."

"But you're from stateside, am I right?" Mr. O'Brian asked.

"Yes, but I used to spend my summers here when I was a kid."

"Well then, you've come to the right place." He scratched behind his ear. "You'll find the history of the Hardcastle quite intriguing, I must say."

"Really?"

"Yes, but we won't get into all of that tonight. I'm sure Liam will have many more details to share, and then we'll get together to fill in the blanks."

"Sounds good to me." I was really beginning to warm up to these people.

I turned to respond to a tap on my shoulder. On my other side, there was a dashing young gentleman who was trying to get my attention.

"Hi, I'm David," he said with a disarming smile. "What may I call you?" He was certainly one to turn heads, and I'm not accustomed to having an immediate attraction to anyone. Still, there was something quite disarming about him.

"I'm Annabelle," I managed, hoping I wasn't tripping all over my tongue. He seemed to be in his mid-thirties or a little older; it was hard to tell. Definitely the business type. He was wearing an expensive Armani suit and had his hair cut so that it wasn't too short but had just enough length that it tapered down the back of his neck and curled up right at the collar. Clean-shaven and clearly tall enough to turn anyone's head. As I reached my hand out to shake his, I could feel the roughness of his palms, letting me know that he's a businessman by day, but he also spends plenty of time outdoors. I could see the contour of his muscles underneath his shirt. I thought I would lose it right then and there, but I managed to keep my composure. I let go of his grip a little too quickly, and in his eyes caught that familiar gleam that had all the indications that he knew just what that meant. The blood rushed to my face, and I tried to think of a way to deflect his attention.

"Nice to meet you, Annabelle. I'm guessing that you're not from around here. I make it my business to know everyone in Cable Creek, and I would have remembered if I had met you before."

"I'm here with my grams," I said, nodding my head in her direction.

"Oh, that's your grandmother?" he asked in surprise.

I smiled and nodded, afraid of what would come out of my mouth at that point.

"Everyone knows Mrs. Gladstone." He gave her a cursory nod before turning his attention back to me. "She's been here for as long as anyone can remember. It wouldn't be Cable Creek without her."

Our chat was interrupted when the waiter came by and refilled our drinks. He said something that made Grams and the O'Brians burst into laughter, but I was still focused on David's apparent charms. He had the finesse of the usual player, and I knew that, but he had my attention just the same. I was momentarily lost in his deep blue eyes and couldn't tear my eyes away from them.

"Oh, David," came a call from the other end of the table. I looked over to see a couple of women beckoning for him to join them.

He excused himself with a promise to meet me later before walking over to join them.

Everyone there seemed to know each other well, and I appeared to be the only one out of my element. Frustration and panic were beginning to build up inside of me. Talk about being thrown into the deep end.

Grams leaned over and whispered in my ear. "Relax, dear, your feelings are starting to show."

My eyes widened. "Grams, what are you talking about?" I declared, but I sounded more like a southern belle than someone trying to fit into an Irish dinner party.

"Your American habits are sticking out," she teased and pinched me lightly on the thigh.

"Well, I'm sorry, Grams. I can't hide who I am, but give me time, and I'm sure I'll fit in soon enough."

She giggled a little schoolgirl giggle and then turned her attention to a gentleman who had just entered the room.

"Who's that?" she asked, her forehead pinching up in the middle.

"You're asking me?"

"I've never seen him before. I thought this first night was exclusive to the locals, but he's not from around here."

"Neither am I."

My eyes followed her gaze to see an older gentleman, probably in his late-sixties or seventies. He was wearing a distinguished suit and carrying a briefcase. My first thought was he was probably a lawyer or some financial adviser. I was pretty good at spotting those kinds of people. He stood in the doorway and beckoned to Liam, who nodded his head when he saw him and then excused himself to go and talk to him.

I looked over at Grams and was surprised at what I saw. The man's presence clearly disturbed her. "What's wrong, Grams?"

"I'm not sure," she said quietly, but her eyes remained fixed on the stranger that had entered the room and didn't break away until the door closed and the two men were gone.

I was beginning to wonder about the man as well. It was odd for Grams to react that way to anyone, and especially to a stranger. I began to wonder what was going through her mind. She usually had pretty good instincts about people, but she didn't like this one for some reason. The only thing that pulled my attention away was a loud noise from the other end of the table where Mr. and Mrs. O'Brian were sitting. I turned to see them both in a panic and hurriedly pushing away from the table.

CHAPTER FIVE

"Oh my," someone said as we watched a flurry of salad flying through the air. "What happened?" Everyone at the table was alarmed by the O'Brians' sudden reaction. Mr. O'Brian could barely move but was clearly trying to get away from something underneath.

"You've got bugs in here," he muttered while his hands kept scratching at his arms and legs.

"Bugs?" screamed another woman who suddenly went into a panic as well. "Did you see bugs?" She was already trying to get out of her chair and away from the table.

"What kind of bugs?" Georgina asked. "I hate bugs."

"I just felt some run across my foot," Mr. O'Brian said.

Everyone turned to Mrs. O'Brian. "Did you see anything?"

She shook her head and stared at her husband. "I just reacted because he panicked."

Mr. O'Brian's alarm triggered a mad search by all the guests for whatever had run across his foot, but nothing was found. By the time Liam returned, the room was in an absolute panic.

"What happened?" Liam asked, his voice rising to a high pitch.

"Mr. O'Brian thinks there are bugs in here," I told him.

A loathsome look spread across Liam's face, and I knew exactly what he was thinking. He had put so much into his venture, and it could all be ruined by some tiny, little bugs.

"Why don't all of you follow me," he finally said after regaining his composure. "I'll have my workers take care of it." He quickly ushered us out of the dining hall and back into the great room.

Still flustered, everyone seemed at least a little relieved that no offending pests were found. But, after Mr. O'Brian's quick reaction and his constant scratching, everyone else was sensing something crawling on them too. It was hard to tell if it was his imagination or not.

After a thorough inspection, we were let back in to finish our dinner before going on a tour of the property.

To me, Hardcastle was an impressive tower of secrets. The vaulted ceilings in every room made me feel small and insignificant in light of its history. As we walked through the endless halls and heard the history, I could see the past come to life. In some areas, knights on horseback returning home from a battle, unicorns, and dwarfs leaned more toward fantasy and fairy tales than real life. Still, how Liam painted his word pictures was very real to me.

Down in the caverns built below ground, it felt somewhat like a crypt. The dampness in the stale air gave it a rather spooky feel. In the end, it was everything one would think of in a castle and more. I was thoroughly mesmerized by its grandeur, and something was beginning to stir up inside of me. I wanted this life, but I didn't know how to get it or if I deserved it.

Grams and I chatted a bit after we returned to our room. I could feel her watching me closely, and I wondered what was going on in her mind. She always had something planned, and we never knew until she was ready to reveal it.

"You really enjoyed today, didn't you?" she asked as she slipped under the covers.

"Yes, I did," I said, trying to keep from smiling too much. "It was the perfect way to end the day. All except for that fiasco in the dining room."

"Mr. O'Brian is an old man. He has diabetes and neuropathy. It's quite possible that his neuropathy was acting up, and he didn't really feel anything."

"Oh, I hope so. This is such a wonderful place. I'd hate to see it ruined before it got started just because some old man thought he felt something that really wasn't there."

"Me too," she agreed quietly.

When I thought she had drifted off to sleep, I settled down in a chair by the window to look over my messages. I groaned inside when I saw so many from my office. What could be the problem? I suppose it was a bit naive to think that I could get away without anything happening. I had been telling Peter—one of our law firm's managers—for months that I needed a break, but my words seemed to have fallen on deaf ears. Now that I had finally been able to get away, it seemed he was more determined than ever to get me back.

Over the past two days, he had sent several of the same messages.

Call me.

Where are you?

I hope you get this message.

Contact me as soon as you get this message.

Urgent that you call...

"Why don't you join me next week on some of the tours of Cable Creek?" Grams' words interrupted my thoughts.

"Huh?" I asked, half distracted and mentally debating whether I should call Peter tonight or wait until morning.

"Why don't you go with me on a tour of the town? I think you'll find it interesting."

"Oh yeah, Grams. Sure. Sounds like a good idea."

I didn't understand why she had asked me, but I knew that my Grams had built quite a reputation here in Cable Creek. If I was seriously going to be staying here, I needed her guidance. I cast a gaze at the old woman, barely a blip underneath the covers. She was my only resource here, and those summer vacations I had as a child weren't going to amount to much if I had any chance of making this my home. I was beginning to realize that I knew nothing about how to really live here in this beautiful place, and it was time I learned what it was really like.

I looked back over my messages and knew that something had gone terribly wrong at work. I wasn't ready to face it yet, so I turned the phone off and decided to call back in the morning. Whatever was happening could easily wait until the next day to deal with. I was just beginning to get comfortable with the possibilities of life in Cable Creek, and I didn't want anything to get in the way. Instead, I pulled an old history book off the shelf and settled down in the bay window to read up on life here.

My mind was racing with ideas, and I wondered if I could get a loan from the bank to finance my own castle. It seemed far-fetched, but I was so caught up in the magic of Cable Creek that it was at least worth giving it a try.

It had occurred to me that I should fix up our family home, but my heart was set on doing it all myself, which meant a new castle. I could never imagine running a place as grand as the Hardcastle Hotel. Still, I was sure that if I found a nice small place to fix my eyes on, I could at least make it into a nice little bed and breakfast. I would talk it over with Grams in the morning and perhaps check out the bank's legal possibilities and financing opportunities and see what happens.

The sound ripped right into my dreams. At first, I wasn't sure what I was hearing, but the blood-curdling scream was loud and frightening. It took a moment for me to get my bearings. My dreams had me back in the offices in New York dealing with some uppity client that I would have preferred to get rid of rather than help. But when I glanced over at Grams trying to get out of her bed, I came back to reality quicker than a flash.

"What was that?" she asked as she struggled to sit up in the bed.

"I don't know," I said, mentally trying to slow down my racing heart. "Sounded like someone screaming."

"I know," she said, getting out of the bed. "Let's go see what it was."

"Why don't you stay here while I go check it out?"

She gave me a strange look. "Did you sleep at all last night?" she asked.

Apparently, I had drifted off to sleep while reading and had not yet changed.

"I guess I fell asleep while reading. It was so comfortable in the window."

"That's not good for you, Belle. You need to learn how to take better care of yourself," she scolded.

"Don't worry, Grams. I don't do it too often. It's just that this view from the window was so wonderful, I couldn't pull myself away. I started reading and just fell asleep."

"Yes, it is a magical place, isn't it?"

Another strange sound came from down the hallway, bringing our conversation to a halt. It sounded like people rushing past our door.

"Something is definitely going on out there, and it doesn't sound good," she said with a worried look on her face.

"Since I'm already dressed, I'll go check it out and let you know." Curiosity was getting the better of me, so I was already heading toward the door.

The hallway looked clear; when I poked my head out, there was no one to be found, but I could hear voices coming from down the next corridor. I stepped out the door just in time to see Liam come dashing around the corner. His face was white and ashen. He was in such a hurry that he nearly lost his balance as he turned the corner, running full speed in the direction of the screams that had now been reduced to a whimper.

I wanted to ask him what was happening, but one look told me Grams' supposition was correct. Something had gone terribly wrong. I stood there for a moment, wondering what to do, but then I heard what sounded like soft sobs mixed with the soft murmur of hushed voices, and I headed in that direction. I didn't want to go back to the room until I knew what had happened. Grams was surely going to want to know. So, I needed to investigate.

CHAPTER SIX

*a*s I turned the corner into the second hallway, I saw a huddled group of guests standing outside an open door, each one peering inside at some curiosity. I recognized Mrs. O'Brian sitting in a chair placed in an odd place almost right in the middle of the hallway, her shoulders hunched over and her face streaked with tears. Another guest I recognized from last night's dinner was holding her hand and stroking it soothingly.

"What happened?" I asked as I approached.

"It's just terrible, just terrible," the woman said. We hadn't had the chance to meet yet, but I thought I heard someone call her Bernie—maybe short for Bernadette.

"What?" I asked again.

"It's Mr. O'Brian. It must've been a heart attack or something."

A gasp of air escaped my lungs involuntarily. "Oh," was all I was able to say. In my mind, I wondered how I was going to break the news to Grams.

"Poor Mrs. O'Brian," she said while shaking her head softly. "She had gone down for an early breakfast, and when she came back, she found him…just lying there. If only she had been there, she probably could have helped him." The woman dabbed her eyes to wipe away tears I couldn't see. "It's just so….so….tragic," she declared dramatically, and I just stared at her. She cast saddened eyes down on Mrs. O'Brian, feigning sympathy. Still, I found it difficult to buy into her performance for some reason. It was too quick. She could have only learned about it seconds ago, and there was something about the tenor of her voice. I couldn't put my finger on it, but something about all of this didn't ring true, and I already doubted her sincerity.

I studied the woman briefly and wondered why she would be so caring toward someone she had just met and then shook my head to clear away the New York suspicions. *Been in the city too long*, I thought. *I make everyone I meet a suspect, but I have to learn how to think differently if I'm going to stay here in Cable Creek.*

I approached the door and peeked inside. The police

had not yet arrived, so the room was open for everyone to see, though no one dared to walk past the threshold. Right in the middle of the room was Mr. O'Brian, lying on the floor, his body contorted into an unusual position. His fingers were curled up into tight little fists that had only slightly released at the moment of death.

He was still in his bedclothes, but the phone laying on the floor in front of him said a lot about his final moments. What an awful sight it must have been for Mrs. O'Brian to find.

I felt sorry for both of them as I studied the poor man lying there. He looked like he knew something was wrong and was attempting to get to his phone and call for help when he finally lost his battle. He had fallen with his fingers outstretched, only inches away from the one device he thought could give him the help he needed.

I turned away from the sight, wondering just how I was going to tell my grams that one of her dear friends was gone. Bernie was still holding Mrs. O'Brian's hands and feigning sadness, but my instincts were already going into overdrive. My eyes traveled from one image to another, and I felt oddly strange. I couldn't put my finger on it right then, but something about the whole situation bothered me.

I studied the scene again. Mrs. O'Brian was visibly

distraught, and there was no talking to her now, so I turned my attention to Liam, who was returning with the police and paramedics in tow.

"Please, everyone, can I ask you to go back to your rooms now so we can take care of this matter?" The police officer was a young man who didn't look old enough to have the experience necessary to work a case like this.

"Officer…" I looked down at his badge to get his name. "Hanlon. May I be of some assistance?" I offered. "I have a legal background and can help you process the scene."

He looked at me as if I had just asked him if he was from Mars. "No, ma'am," he finally said. "I believe we have everything under control here."

"Pardon me, but you've just arrived. You don't have anything under control. You need to process the scene properly first."

"I'm sorry, but there is nothing to process. From what I can gather and what Mr. Liam told me, he was an old man. It's most likely a heart attack."

The hairs on the back of my neck started to stand up. "Oh, and you're basing this on what facts?" I blurted out. "You haven't even examined the crime scene." I locked eyes with him. "I don't believe this was a heart attack."

Officer Hanlon looked as if he had been slapped.

Then he looked as if he had been entertained. "And what are you basing your deductions on?" he asked with more than a little derision in his voice. Then he gave me a mocking smile that curled up at the corner of his lips.

"It just doesn't look like a heart attack," I finally said, choosing to ignore his disrespectful tone. "If he had a heart attack, he would have been clutching his chest, but instead, he's clutching his stomach. His face is contorted, like he was in excruciating pain. Even from here, I can see the deep cuts in the palms of his hands, most likely from digging his fingernails in. It's easy to see that he was suffering."

"Well, why don't you leave the detective work to us professionals," he said dismissively. Then he brushed past me, clapped his hands together loudly to get everyone's attention, and told them to go back to their rooms again.

"Why don't I take Mrs. O'Brian back to my room with me," I finally suggested, knowing I was going to get nowhere with this one. If I wanted to help, I'd need to talk to someone higher up than this man.

"I think she should stay here," he objected. "We might have to ask her some questions."

I rolled my eyes. "Listen, this is a seventy-year-old woman whose husband has just died here in this hotel room. Her room. All her things are here, the body of her husband of forty years is just a few feet away, and she has no one at home waiting for her. I can assure you, she's not going anywhere. My room is just around this corner. I think she should wait there with my grandmother, her dearest friend, so she can have someone to take care of her and help her get through this. If you need to ask her any questions, the room number is two-one-two; you can just knock. One of us will let you in. We're not going anywhere."

I looked again at poor Mr. O'Brian lying there on the floor and shook my head. I had talked to him a few hours earlier, and he seemed absolutely fine. He was laughing and joking with Grams and being a perfect guest for this fabulous hotel, and now he was gone. What could have happened?

Not waiting for an answer from Hanlon, I took her hand from Bernie, pulled her gently to her feet, and together we started walking down the hallway toward our room. She seemed even frailer than my grams, but I wasn't sure why. Maybe it was because of the trauma she had just experienced, or she was just usually a tiny person. Together we walked slowly down the hall, her hand gripping mine so tightly my fingers started to tingle. She was a strong one for such a tiny person.

As we passed, I studied the faces of all the people in the hallways. I was sure that they couldn't have all been guests of the hotel. We only had a group of about twenty but there were many more than that gathered now. Some were there simply for the excitement and maybe a little bit of gossip. Others just appeared to be curious, but none seemed to be genuinely interested in the O'Brians. Clearly, everyone was distraught about what had happened but not necessarily saddened by the tragic ending. Suddenly, the story of the Hardcastle was a very different one, and it was going to take some doing for it to live down this terrible event. Cable Creek had a lasting reputation for small-town gossip, and I could already see the writing on the wall.

CHAPTER SEVEN

I knocked on the door before I used my key card to enter. When I opened it, I found Grams already up and dressed. She was sitting at the old-fashioned vanity table situated between the two windows, brushing her hair. I saw the look of surprise in her reflection in the mirror when she saw her dear friend coming in with me.

"Oh my!" she exclaimed with joy, and then, noticing the distraught look on Mrs. O'Brian's face, and no doubt, the tear-stained streaks, her expression suddenly changed. She made a quizzical glance in my direction before she asked, "What's this?"

"Grams, something awful has happened, and I brought Mrs. O'Brian here to get away from all the craziness."

"What craziness?" she asked, her perplexed look darting from my face to her friend's.

"Mr. O'Brian died this morning."

It took only a few seconds for my words to sink in. The point was driven home by a small, barely audible whisper from Mrs. O'Brian before she fell silent again.

I walked her over to the sofa and helped her ease into a seat. "Can I get you anything?" I asked, unsure what the protocol was for this kind of situation. She shook her head back and forth before burying her face in her trembling hands and sobbing quietly. I patted her on her forearm. "I'm so sorry for your loss," I muttered. "I'll be right back." Even as I said it, I felt like it was inappropriate but I was out of my element.

I didn't know if it was okay to leave her alone, but I had to fill Grams in on what had happened. She was still standing there with a stunned look on her face.

"What happened?" she asked when I came over to talk with her.

"I don't know exactly, but I think something is not quite right," I told her.

"What happened?" she asked again.

"Apparently, Mr. O'Brian didn't want an early breakfast so she went down alone. When she returned to the room, she found him face down on the floor. They called paramedics, but it looks like they came too late. I saw them come in and as far as I can tell, they didn't make any attempt to revive him. They are with him now."

"Oh, how sad," Grams said. "The two have been together for so long. I don't know what she's gonna do. She'll be lost without him."

I felt the soft buzz of my cell phone in my pocket and remembered I was supposed to call the office this morning. "Grams, I need to take this call. Why don't you sit with her, and I'll step out in the hallway." I turned as I headed toward the door. "If I get any more news while I'm out there, I'll let you know."

Grams just gave me a nod and hurried to console her friend.

I opened my phone and answered. "Hold on, Peter. Let me get to someplace where we can talk. There are too many people around now."

The hallway was filled with even more people now. As I walked past, each one was whispering their opinions about what might have happened.

"Poor man, must've had a heart attack. He wasn't that healthy, you know."

"I guess he's been going downhill for a long time."

"I don't know. I thought he was pretty strong for his age."

"How old do you think he was?"

"I don't know, maybe seventy. Not sure."

"He seemed fine last night. Remember when he jumped out of his chair? He moved like a much younger man."

"That's true, but he was a smoker for many years. It's a wonder cancer didn't get to him."

"I wonder what's going to happen to his estate."

"What estate?"

"They own an estate way out on the outskirts of town. Beautiful spot overlooking the sea."

"I heard someone was trying to buy it from them, but he didn't want to sell."

"Can't blame him. Those kinds of places are hard to find."

It seemed everyone had an opinion, so I kept walking until I was well out of earshot of all the guests. This meant I had to make my way down the stairs before I could actually speak.

"Hello," I said into the phone as I headed for the main entrance.

I heard Peter's exasperated voice on the other end: "Annabelle. Finally. What is going on out there?"

"Peter, why are you bothering me? You know I'm on vacation."

"I know, I know. And I wouldn't be bothering you if it wasn't important. We finally got a ruling on your

Cassidy case." The Cassidy case was one I had been working on for going on three years. Tony Cassidy was a wealthy businessman who had been caught withholding his earnings from the IRS. He had asked our firm to help him avoid paying a hefty penalty or jail time for not reporting his earnings. We had been playing dodge with the system for years.

"You're kidding," I breathed into the phone as I pushed open the main entrance door to go outside.

"Yes, finally. We have a court date for next Thursday. Can you be back by then?"

I was incredulous. "Peter, I just got here. There's no way I can be back by Thursday."

"Tony only wants to work with you. I'm sorry, but we need you."

"No can do, Peter. I told you before I left that I needed some well-deserved time off…"

"And I told him just that, but he insisted."

I had reached halfway down the outside steps before Liam caught up with me. "I'm sorry, Annabelle, but I need you to come back inside."

"Excuse me, Peter…" I placed the phone on my chest and looked at Liam. "Why? What's wrong?"

"The police don't want anyone leaving until they finish their investigation."

"Investigation? I thought it was a heart attack," I said, but I wasn't completely surprised by the decision.

"Well, that's the preliminary assessment, but they still want to do an investigation just to make sure."

"I'm not going anywhere; I'm just going to walk around the garden so I can take my phone call without being disturbed."

"I'm sorry, but right now, even the garden is off-limits. You are free to use my office if that helps."

I couldn't say how frustrating it was for me. I didn't understand why going outside was going to be a problem. After all, I had nothing to do with the O'Brians. Grams and I weren't even in the same part of the hotel.

"I'm sorry, Peter," I said into the phone. "I have to go now. We're having a...an issue here at the moment."

"But what are we going to do about the Cassidy case?"

"Give it to Betty. I'm sure she can handle it."

"But Tony said he only wanted to work with you."

"I know he did. But if he wants to stay out of prison, he'll accept help from Betty or you. You didn't get to be the manager of a huge law firm simply by accepting whatever the client wants. Where's your backbone? Please, you know I need this time off, and my grams needs me right now. I can't come back now. I just can't; I'm sorry."

I could hear him sucking in his breath so he could launch another complaint, but I hung up before he could say another word. Reluctantly, I gave Liam a nod and followed him back to the hotel's main entrance.

By the time we had climbed the stairs back to the room, they were taking poor Mr. O'Brian's body out on a stretcher. Liam was called to the side to talk to Officer Hanlon. Since we had been walking together, I made the choice to stick with him. I didn't ask, and no one objected.

"Officer." I nodded as we approached.

"Ma'am," he responded curtly.

"So, is everything resolved?" Liam asked, his voice wavering just a bit. I felt bad for him. What an awful tragedy on the first day he opens up this beautiful new hotel.

"Yes, it looks like a pretty open and shut case."

"What do you think happened?"

"We have a white male, seventy-two years old; my guess…probably a heart attack."

"I thought there would be an investigation?" I asked.

"Maybe, but we can't say for sure. As it stands now, I don't see any evidence of foul play here."

"How do you know?" I asked. "Mrs. O'Brian will want some answers."

He pulled off his hat and rubbed his forehead, not even trying to hide his frustration. "She has her answer."

"Are you at least going to have his body examined and an autopsy done?"

He scrunched up his brow. "In cases like this, we don't usually order an autopsy. Unless Mrs. O'Brian asks for one, none will be done." He turned his attention to Liam as if to completely dismiss me, but I refused to accept this as the end for Mr. O'Brian. Mrs. O'Brian was a dear friend of my grams, and I wasn't about to let this just drop until I could get as many questions answered as I could.

"How do you know?" I asked, showing a little of my own irritation.

"Ma'am, we are trained to identify a dead body."

"Are you a coroner or a medical doctor? You may know what dead looks like, but do you have the background or experience to determine the cause?"

"The man was over seventy years old. What do you think happened to him?" He nearly spat his words at me.

"I don't know," I snapped back at him. "But, what I do know is that I don't know everything. I am willing to get a doctor's opinion about the cause of death. And I don't believe you have the qualifications to do that."

"Like I said, it is out of our hands now. Unless Mrs. O'Brian orders an autopsy, or the preliminary cause of death reveals anything out of the ordinary, there is nothing more that we can do."

"Have you talked to Mrs. O'Brian?"

"Yes, briefly. I just left her. She's with your grandmother now. I told her to try to get some rest, and we can finalize everything in the morning."

"Hmf." I snorted and folded my arms. I had nothing to say to him at the moment, but I still felt like something wasn't quite right.

"Is the room clear?" Liam asked.

"For now," he said. "I wouldn't let anyone in there until we get the official all-clear, which will probably be sometime tomorrow."

"Really? Do you think there'll be an investigation?"

Hanlon gave me a hard stare before he gave Liam his answer.

"I don't expect any long drawn-out investigation, but we do have to follow protocol. Once we get the official cause of death, we'll know how to proceed from there."

Liam looked partially relieved, but I could still see the worry lines etched in his forehead.

I regarded Hanlon. "Mind if I take a look around in there? I'm sure Mrs. O'Brian will need some of her things," I offered.

Hanlon looked like he wasn't sure what to do. "I suppose you can enter as long as you have one of the officers escort you. I can't stress enough how important it is to not take anything out of the room until we have finished processing the scene."

"What about Mrs. O'Brian? Can she take her things out?"

"Nothing," he said before he turned and walked away, ending the discussion.

"Thank you," Liam called after him. "Thank you for taking care of this so quickly." His tone didn't show much relief. He was saying all the right things, but he seemed worried.

Hanlon nodded his head and beckoned for one of his officers to join us, the rest following him as they left the building.

I stared after them until they had gone down the stairs and out of my line of vision.

"I'm going to go check the room," Liam said.

"Mind if I join you?"

He looked like he was thinking about it, but he finally agreed.

"I just want to see for myself if everything is back to normal," I told him. "I want to give real answers to Grams and to Mrs. O'Brian when I go back to the room."

He nodded and the three of us climbed the stairs and quietly walked down the hall to their room.

CHAPTER EIGHT

*T*he door to the O'Brians' room was still open, but there was yellow tape strung across the entry, so you couldn't just walk in. We waited for the officer to remove the tape, and I followed Liam inside. I stood in the middle of the large room and just tried to soak in everything I saw. Everything seemed to be in order. The sliding door to the balcony was slightly ajar, but otherwise, everything looked just as it should.

"Don't touch anything," the officer said firmly. He didn't seem to be speaking to me directly, but I had the feeling that I was the one he was talking to. I nodded that I understood and walked into the bedroom area. It felt like their life had come to a complete stop and every moment was frozen in time. Their open suitcases were on the bed along with a medicine bag filled with at least twenty bottles of prescription medications, some for Mr. O'Brian and the others for Mrs. O'Brian.

"Who carries this much medicine for one overnight stay?" I asked.

"I heard that he had been pretty sick," the officer said. "Maybe he needed them."

"Maybe. Seems like a bit of overkill, but what do I know?"

I tried to read the labels, but I couldn't make heads or tails of them. I didn't know much about medication, but I did remember someone saying something about his neuropathy. I didn't know what that was either.

"So," Liam said as he came into the bedroom where I was trying to look through Mr. O'Brian's suitcase without touching anything. "Why are you so sure that something happened to him?"

I looked up quickly. "I work in law. I'm not a criminal lawyer or anything like that, but when you're around all sorts of people, you quickly learn that everything is not always what it seems."

"Did you hear anything, or did you notice something off?"

I didn't want to tell him that I knew for sure what had happened, but I was convinced that the situation was being handled poorly by the police.

"No, nothing concrete that I can put my finger on...

at least not yet. I'm just following a hunch now, but I usually have a pretty good sense about these things."

"Anything you want to share with me?"

"No, not yet. I need to process all this first, and then I'll let you know what I'm thinking."

I walked over to the bathroom. The counter was covered with all the things you would expect an elderly person to have. His dentures were still in a cup on the counter right alongside a package of Denture Grip. Nothing unusual here.

"What are you looking for?" Liam asked. I could tell he wasn't quite sure what to make of me.

"I'm not sure. I'll know it when I see it."

The bathroom looked perfectly fine, except for some yellow specks that appeared to have been splattered on the wall and the mirror. They were tiny flecks of something I couldn't quite make out, but I could see nothing in the room that would have caused it.

"What's this?" I asked Liam.

He came over and studied the splatter pattern carefully. "I have no idea," he answered. "What do you think it is?"

"I don't know, but I would guess that it's not hotel standard."

"That I know for sure."

I walked over and examined everything spread out

on the counter. There I found all of Mrs. O'Brian's things. Her cosmetics, a bottle of perfume, and a medical ID tag.

"You know," I said, "I think Mrs. O'Brian is going to need that medical ID tag. Mind if I bring it to her?"

The officer's eyes perked up. "Nothing is to be touched."

"But she's an old woman. She needs it, especially now. What if she has a medical episode and there is no medical alert. It could delay getting the care she needs."

He looked confused. You could almost see the wheels turning in his head trying to decide what to do.

"Listen," I said, "you can catalogue it, photograph it, log it into inventory, whatever, but how could you deprive her of this life-saving device? Especially in a situation where you're not even sure that there's a crime involved..." I picked up the bracelet and walked over to him. "See, there is nothing here except an emergency alarm button to press if she has a medical emergency. Nothing more."

"Well, I guess that would be okay," he said reluctantly. His face showed a slight hint of fear but he nodded his head in agreement. I slipped the tag into my pocket and went over to join Liam.

"So, why are you determined to push for an investigation?" Liam asked me.

I could tell he was anxious for all of this to be finished but he was walking in unfamiliar territory.

"Like I said, I'm a lawyer. I'm a stickler for details and looking for things that are less than obvious. It may not be anything, but it doesn't hurt to examine everything carefully just to make sure."

"I guess so," he said quietly as he closed the door to the balcony and locked it. "But as far as I can tell, there is nothing out of the ordinary here."

I plopped down in the window seat by the fireplace and let my thoughts run wild. "My grams and the O'Brians have been friends since they were children, and I know how much she cares about them. I also know how important it would be to both of them that his death not be swept under the rug. Mr. O'Brian was an important member of this community, and his death will be a loss for most of the people here in Cable Creek. I feel I owe it to my grams and Mrs. O'Brian to make sure that everything is right before this whole matter is put to rest."

The whole morning had been confusing, and I needed to find a way to put it right. "And besides," I mumbled out loud, "I just have to wonder why the police are so determined to close the book on this so fast."

"I guess that is partly my fault," he confessed. "I kind

of pushed him to close it fast. The Hardcastle hasn't officially opened yet, and I'm afraid that any negative news would kill our reputation before we got it off the ground. It would be devastating for my business. You understand that, don't you?"

I nodded, but I wasn't sure I agreed with him. Pressuring the police to ignore what could be a dire situation may be the way things are done in Cable Creek, but that wasn't what I was used to. The matter needed to be investigated.

"Well, I don't see much to worry about here," I finally said. "As far as I can tell there is nothing out of the ordinary so you may be in the clear. Let's go and talk to Mrs. O'Brian."

CHAPTER NINE

The atmosphere in our room was solemn. Since I had left, several people had stopped in to offer their condolences to Mrs. O'Brian. Some she knew from her past, but others had no idea who she was. In Cable Creek, news traveled quickly.

When we entered, a small group had gathered in the center living area, sitting by the fire and chatting quietly amongst themselves, but Mrs. O'Brian was nowhere to be seen.

"She's resting," someone told me when she saw me looking around for her.

"Where?" I asked, wanting to talk to her one-on-one.

"In the room next door. I thought it was best."

I nodded my head but wondered at the same time who had the room next door. It hadn't even been a

thought before, but now it felt like it was more important than ever.

I stared at all the people who had gathered in our
room and wondered what their connection was with the
O'Brians. I recognized some of them from the dinner
the night before, but the others were complete
strangers. Considering what had just happened, getting
to know all of these people was not something to be
ignored.

Liam came and stood next to me. For a minute, he
said nothing, looking a little out of sorts once again.

"Why don't I order up some food for you guys," he
offered. "On the house, of course. It's the least I can do."

I suppose he was right. It seemed that we had
become the honorary hosts for the O'Brians. Once
people learned what had happened, it was only logical
that they would come here, especially knowing that
Mrs. O'Brian would be here with us for the time being.

"I guess the rest of the events for the weekend are
off," said a tall woman who had been a part of the group,
but I hadn't had the chance to meet yet. Her comment
was addressed to Liam, and I detected a hint of disappointment in her tone.

"I'm so sorry about this, Rebecca. It would be hard to
keep the spirit of things up for now. I'll be happy to give
you a rain check," he offered.

"Don't worry, I understand. I'm just so happy that this didn't happen on your official opening night, Liam. I can't imagine what I would do if this happened at my place on the first day I was open for business."

"Do you have a place too?" I interjected. Especially since they were talking as if I wasn't even there.

"No, no, no," Rebecca said with a laugh. "I'm just a travel agent here. Liam invited me in hopes of getting me to promote his place when it officially opens."

"I'm so sorry, Annabelle. I should've introduced you. Rebecca, this is Annabelle. She is here from the States, visiting her grandmother here in Cable Creek. Annabelle, this is Rebecca. She runs the number-one travel agency this side of town."

"Wow, impressive. Nice to meet you, Rebecca. Did you know the O'Brians before this trip?"

"No, not me personally. My husband was doing some business with Mr. O'Brian, but I wasn't really a part of it."

"Oh, is your husband here now?" I asked, curious to meet him.

"Yeah, he's around here somewhere." She stuck her long neck out even further to scan the group but apparently didn't see him. "Maybe he stepped out for a bit. He's had to field a lot of business calls this morning."

"Because of his dealings with Mr. O'Brian?"

"I guess. I don't know much about what he does. You'll have to ask him when he returns."

"Well, if you ladies will excuse me," Liam said, "I'll arrange for some food to be brought up."

"Okay, thank you," I said rather absentmindedly. I barely heard what he had said; I was deep in my own thoughts. But as soon as he walked away, Rebecca's tone changed.

"So," she started. I knew that tone, and I knew which direction she was heading even before it started. "You and Liam? Nice match."

I didn't know what to say. It came out of left field, and I had no idea where she'd gotten that idea.

"No, of course not. I just met him last night. I don't know anything about him."

"You don't have to hide it from me. I saw the two of you this morning heading out to the garden. I knew there was something between you two. Trust me, you can't keep something like that a secret around here for too long."

"I can assure you there is nothing going on between Liam and me. I didn't even know the man before yesterday, and the only thing he knows about me is that my grandmother is a very well-known person here in Cable Creek. You're mistaken. Liam was just talking to me about not leaving the hotel until the police finished their investigation. That's all, nothing more." I was afraid that my tone would have hurt her feelings. I had a tendency to be cold and sharp when irritated, and this woman was already getting under my skin.

"That's right, I heard that you were here visiting your grandmother. Do I know her? Who is she?"

"You probably do. My grandmother is probably in the Who's Who book of Ireland. She knows everybody. Mrs. Clarissa Gladstone."

Rebecca gasped. "Oh my, that's your grandmother? Of course, I know her. If you want to get anywhere, do anything, or learn about anyone in Cable Creek, Clarissa is the one to go to."

I had to chuckle a little bit. "You got that right."

We were momentarily distracted when the door opened again and the room fell silent. I looked up to see the same strange man I had seen at the dinner the night before. He seemed to be wearing the same suit he had on the night before but I couldn't be sure. He looked around the room, staring at each guest as if he was searching for someone, then he turned and walked out again.

"Who is that man?" I asked.

"Beats me," Rebecca said. "Never saw him before."

"Strange. I saw him last night, too. He looks like he is looking for someone."

"Maybe," she said dismissively. "So, how long are you staying here in Ireland?"

"I don't know," I answered honestly. "I have an open-ended ticket, and I'd like to stay as long as possible."

"You won't go wrong with that. This is truly a magical place."

"I couldn't have said it better myself."

I let my eyes scan the room. Every few minutes, people were coming in and out. It was a far cry from what I was expecting. "Will you excuse me a minute?" I asked her. "I think I want to go and check on Mrs. O'Brian."

"That's a good idea. Mind if I join you?"

I scrunched up my face a little. "I'd rather I went alone for now. I don't know how well she is handling everything. She might be feeling overwhelmed."

"No worries, I understand," she said, her eyes already scanning the room for someone else to talk to. "Give her my regards."

Outside there were even more people gathered. It was hard to make my way past all the people who had collected just outside the door. I just wanted to get to the next room, but it was almost impossible with the number of people who had arrived, and it seemed as if they were still coming. This is what small-town living is like, I guess.

"Excuse me," I kept saying as I pushed through the growing crowd. Surely, all these people were not guests of the hotel. I wondered where they'd come from and how the news had gotten out so fast.

Finally, I managed to get through the crowd and made my way to the room next door. I knocked softly, hoping that whoever answered would recognize me and let me in. The door opened, and I was never so happy to see anyone in my life.

"Hey, Annabelle," Spencer said with a look of relief on his face.

"Hey, Spencer, what are you doing here? Were you a guest here last night?"

"No, I'm nobody. Your grams just called and asked if I could help. Come on inside."

The room was identical to ours. The same spacious layout but with a divider to separate the two sleeping areas from the common space.

"This is nice," I commented as I looked around the room.

"Wish I could afford something like this. But that may never be within my reach."

"You never know, Spencer. You never know what's possible."

He just nodded his head as if he had heard those

expressions a thousand times before and decided it wasn't worth the debate.

I smiled and turned the conversation to my purpose for being there. "I came to check on Mrs. O'Brian. How's she doing?"

"A little overwhelmed, I think, but bearing up."

"Did the police come to talk to her?"

"No, not really. They just stopped by to tell her they were taking the body to the hospital and that she should come to the station tomorrow to finish filing the report."

I wasn't surprised at their lack of interest, but I thought they would have had a little more decency than treating it as a simple matter of paperwork. "Where is she?" I asked, looking around the room.

"She's in there." He pointed to the divider that led to one of the sleeping areas. "With your grams."

"Thank you."

I knocked softly on the makeshift door and waited. A feeble voice said, "Come in." It was only then that I opened the door and went inside. The two of them were sitting on the small window seat overlooking the gardens.

"I came to check to see how you were doing," I said quietly. "Is there anything I can do for you?"

The two of them sat there quietly. At first glance, you

would think they were as frail as leaves blowing in the autumn wind, and the first hint of adversity would blow them away. But I knew better. If Mrs. O'Brian was anything like my grams, they were both formidable women, and Lord help anyone who thought differently.

"No, I'm okay for now," Mrs. O'Brian said, her voice sounding much stronger than I had expected.

"I know this must be hard for you, but I'd like to help in any way I can."

She patted my hand softly. "What can you do? He's already gone, and no one is going to bring him back to me."

"I know, but I just want to know that everything has been done the right way."

"I know you mean well, child, but this is the way of life when you get to be our age."

I reached in my pocket and pulled out the emergency alert chain. "I know this is difficult, but I thought you might need this. I found it in your room."

"What is it?" she asked, reaching for it with trembling fingers.

"It's your medical alert chain."

"No, it's not mine," she said. "I have mine on right here. We're supposed to keep it on at all times." She pulled at the chain around her neck. "Me and Patrick never take them off."

I grabbed the chain and examined it a little more closely. "Could it have been your husband's?"

"No, I don't think so. We got ours at the same time. They're identical. See?" She pointed to the logo on the back. "This is the agency that monitors them. That one is different."

She was right. The logo was different.

"Was anyone else in your room last night?" I asked.

"No, it was just Patrick and me. We usually retire early, so we came up right after the tour yesterday and settled in for the night."

My mind was racing. Had someone been in their room that morning? That's what I needed to find out.

"How about this morning?" I pushed a little harder.

"Not while I was there. I suppose someone could have come while I was down to breakfast, but I was gone for less than half an hour. I can't imagine anyone would have been able to visit in that short amount of time. He was still in bed when I left."

I had more questions but I didn't want to push too hard. Obviously, someone else had been in their room and had left this medical alert device. It seemed an odd thing to do but I just couldn't figure it out right then.

"Tomorrow," I said, "you have to go to the police department to finish the report?"

"Yes."

"I'd like to go with you if you don't mind."

"I'd love that. I don't know how I will get through it if I have to go there alone."

Grams sucked in on her teeth. "Don't be silly, Lillian. We would never let you do something like that alone. I know how hard it is to go through that. I wouldn't think of you doing that by yourself."

CHAPTER TEN

 t was a relief to get back to Gladstone. I was never so happy to see those towers in my life. The night at the Hardcastle Hotel had been both exhilarating and frightening. My legalese mind had taken over and gotten the better of me. I was afraid I had made the worst first impression possible.

In my room, I finally had time to think. I had left New York to get away from all the hassles of city life, and it felt like I had just been thrown right back into it. Still, here I seemed to be able to cope much better with the craziness; it was not as intense as it would be in a big city. No, they were the same white-collar people I had to deal with, but their lives had their own flair. They reflected a world that I genuinely wanted to be a part of.

I thought about my own family line, and I wondered

what kind of courage it took to take on a venture like building your own castle. Could I do that? It was an attractive thought, no doubt about it. Liam's Hardcastle Hotel was grand enough to impress anybody. I wasn't sure I could do anything on that level, but maybe I could find a suitable property and build a little something on my own. I was sure I could handle something small and intimate.

But for now, my thoughts had to go back to Mrs. O'Brian. She had been through a terrible ordeal, and I wasn't so sure she was out of it. When we finally had the all-clear to return home, we brought her home with us. It just wouldn't have been good to let her go back to that big rambling house all alone, so Grams set her up in the room next to mine. That way, I could keep an eye on both of them.

Now, back in my room alone, I could mentally break down everything that had happened since I'd been there. For the first time, I was able to open up my computer and catch up on everything going on back in the States. But my eagerness to get down to business dissipated when I realized that there were more than two hundred emails I needed to answer. Most of them were from Peter. I couldn't deal with that now, so I sent him a quick reply, telling him to delegate my work because I would need more time than I'd initially thought. Then I quickly shut it down again, and this time, I crawled in the bed and went to sleep.

The next morning, Grams gave me her car to drive Mrs. O'Brian to the police station. I thought it was really insensitive of them to make her come down to the station rather than them coming to her. The thought of that Officer Hanlon really irritated me. I hoped that it wasn't him we were going to talk to; I didn't know just how well I could contain my temper if he started talking down to me again.

The police station was just as drab as the men who worked there. It was an old building with little lighting. Even if you wanted to see the detailed craftsmanship of the old building, you couldn't. It looked like they had installed only 40-watt bulbs in the whole place, which gave the room a dirty yellow look. As soon as we entered, there was a reception desk, and an older man was stationed there. He looked like this was his last stop before retirement, and they didn't know where else to place him.

"May I help you?" he asked, barely acknowledging our presence.

"Yes, this is Lillian O'Brian. She's come here to finish up some paperwork on her husband's death."

The man suddenly came to attention. "Oh, Mrs. O'Brian," he said, his tone now much gentler. "I was so sorry to hear about your husband. It must be a very difficult time for you."

"Did you know Patrick?" she asked.

"Yes, yes, I did. Patrick and I go way back. We served together in the army. We stayed in touch for years, and then, for some reason, we lost contact. Maybe he's mentioned me before. I'm Sean Callahan."

Mrs. O'Brian scrunched up her brow, trying to remember. "Not that I recall," she told him, "but I have to admit, I'm not thinking that clearly right now. Maybe you can come for a visit after everything has settled down, and we'll figure it out then."

"Sounds like a plan to me," he said with a smile.

"The report?" I reminded him. I wanted to get the whole thing over as soon as possible.

"Oh, yes. Sergeant Collins is waiting for you in his office. Just go through those double doors there, and it's the first door on your left."

It was nice to chat with someone so pleasant. I was beginning to have a different viewpoint of the Cable Creek police force.

Collins' office was a little brighter than the main waiting area. Instead of the dingy lighting, he had nice open windows that let in lots of natural sunlight. His office was furnished with a well-polished mahogany desk and what looked like an ergonomic desk chair. I was sure he had put on all the finishing touches himself, or maybe it was his wife.

He ushered us in and politely gave us a seat before he settled his bulky shape into his own contoured luxury chair.

"Can I get you anything before we get started?" he asked.

We both shook our heads now.

"Well," he said. "First, I want to apologize for how my men handled your husband's demise yesterday."

Another surprise for me.

"You have to understand, Cable Creek is a small, family community. Cases like this are not very common, and I hate to admit it, but many of my men are not trained to handle these types of situations."

"I understand," Mrs. O'Brian said softly.

He reached for a file from a pack of many and opened it up. He paused for a second while he collected his thoughts. When he did speak, he spoke to me first and not to Mrs. O'Brian. "I understand that you, Ms. Shannon, had some objections to how the case was handled yesterday."

I was surprised by his directness and was momentarily speechless.

"The reason I bring it up is that we were wondering if you knew more about what happened to Mr. O'Brian than you led my officers to believe."

Again I was stunned. "I'm not sure what you're asking," I finally started. "I had only met the O'Brians the night before at dinner. I can't imagine that I would know anything more about them than what they shared with us that night."

"Well, some of the other guests said that you all seemed rather chummy the night before."

"Of course we were," I said a little too defensively. "They are very good friends of my grams. You may know her…Clarissa Gladstone."

He scoffed, then smiled. "Everyone knows Clarissa, but that's not what I'm getting at."

"Well, I wish you'd explain yourself a little more clearly because I'm not sure what you're talking about. Are you trying to accuse me of something?"

Mrs. O'Brian seemed to focus and listen to the conversation for the first time. "What? What are you trying to say?" she asked.

"Nothing really, Mrs. O'Brian. We're just trying to connect the dots, that's all."

"I thought my husband died of a heart attack."

"That may well be true, but we won't know that until an autopsy is performed."

"An autopsy? Why do you need an autopsy?" A hint of alarm was rising in her voice.

"It's standard procedure when the cause of death is not readily apparent."

"But that's what your officers told me yesterday when they...when they..."

"That is the general assumption for now, but we can't close the case until we get a determination from the medical examiner."

"So, what do you have now?" I asked, trying to lean over and look at the file.

"Nothing much. He was found lying face down on the floor of his hotel room. It appeared that he could have had some medical condition that may have been the cause of death or at least contributed to it. Mrs. O'Brian, did your husband have any underlying health issues that we should be aware of?"

"Yes. He has a pacemaker and was a diabetic. He also suffered from peripheral neuropathy, which caused him a lot of discomfort. But it wasn't like he was suffering so much that he couldn't live an active life. He was in good spirits at the hotel, and he wasn't having any problems that night."

"Good to know," he said, making notes in his file.

"Good to know. So, can you run through what happened that morning?"

"Excuse me," I interrupted. "Is there a reason why you are asking these questions now and not yesterday when your detectives should have done a proper investigation?"

He snapped the file closed and looked directly at me. "Yes, I can Ms. Shannon. Yesterday, we were called simply to accompany the paramedics to a medical emergency. No crime was reported, so no investigation was needed."

His answer seemed logical, but it only brought up more questions in my mind. "But apparently you've learned something since then because clearly, you're doing an investigation now."

He leaned back in his chair and looked directly at me. "I can see why Detective Hanlon was so perturbed when he spoke with you."

"You still haven't answered my question."

There was a long pause before he spoke again. "Yes, there were some discrepancies in the case, but I can't disclose them to you now."

"I see. So can you at least tell us why you are questioning Mrs. O'Brian? She was under the impression that she was here to fill out a report from yesterday."

"We're just trying to connect the dots, that's all. And

if you would allow her to speak, we could probably get this done much quicker. Is that okay?"

His kind demeanor had changed, and I worried that I may have just made things worse for her.

"I just have one more question, if I may."

He gestured with his hands for me to continue. I got the feeling that he just wanted me to hurry up so he could get it all over with.

"Did Mr. O'Brian have his medical alert chain around his neck?"

The question seemed to catch him by surprise. He opened the file again and scanned its pages. "I don't know," he said after a long time. He looked over at Mrs. O'Brian. "Does he wear a medical alert chain?"

"Yes, he never takes it off."

He scanned the file again. "That's interesting. I'll have to check with the coroner and the paramedics before I can answer that."

I reached in my pocket and pulled out the medical alert chain I had found in the bathroom of the O'Brians' hotel room. "I found this one in the bathroom of their room." I laid it on the desk for him to see. "Mrs. O'Brian says this is not her husband's medical alert, but no one came to visit them while she was there."

He picked up the chain and examined it but didn't

say anything more. Finally, he asked, "How did you get this?"

"I was with Liam and your officer to check the room yesterday after your officers left."

"You shouldn't have taken anything from the room."

"Your officer said as much when I talked to him. But I was under the impression that it belonged to Mrs. O'Brian and it was something she needed." I paused and waited for a response and when none came, I continued, "The officer that escorted us agreed."

"Do you know the officer's name?"

"No, but I'd know him if I saw him."

"All right," he said quietly through clenched teeth.

"So, what do you think this means?" I asked, my curiosity getting the better of me.

"I suppose that someone visited him while Mrs. O'Brian was having breakfast."

"But the question still remains. Who was it, and why did they leave this device behind?"

"Hmm," was all he said, and slipped the alert tag into his top drawer.

CHAPTER ELEVEN

We finally walked out of the police station an hour later, and I took Mrs. O'Brian over to the mortuary to discuss funeral arrangements. She had proven to be much stronger than I'd imagined. She had every detail of his service clear in her head, and the weeping senior citizen I had observed the night before was more like a stalwart warrior today. I wasn't quite sure what to make of this change.

Was she like my grams, take care of business because there was little time to feel sorry for yourself, or was there a little coldness in her? I couldn't quite put my finger on it just yet. I excused myself to let her finalize the arrangements on her own so I could use the time to call Grams and see how she was doing.

Grams was busy and had little time to chat, so I decided to use the time to take care of one dreaded task. I had to call Peter and clear things up with him. I knew he had no idea what was going on here, and I had left him a little confused from our last conversation. I went back to the car to do this because I wasn't sure what kind of reaction I would get, and I didn't want anyone else around if he lost it. Besides, I had already learned how quickly news traveled here in Cable Creek, and I didn't want to add any fuel to the fire or foster any misunderstandings.

My call was put right through, and he answered on the first ring. A bad sign.

"Annabelle," he nearly shouted into the phone.

"Hey, Peter, what's going on there?"

"Everything. You already know what's going on with the Cassidy case and…well, it seems like as soon as you left, everything just went up in smoke. We need you back here as soon as possible."

I gave him a frustrated grunt. Is this the way all men are? It seems they never listen.

"Listen, Peter, I told you I needed some time off. I can't just come back every time something happens."

"I know you deserve this vacation; you really do. But why did you have to go so far away? Why couldn't you take your vacation somewhere closer to home?"

"Ireland is my home. My family has been from here for generations."

"That's not what I mean, and you know it." He was clearly getting angry.

Exasperated, I had to hold my breath for a few seconds. "Listen, Peter, I haven't had a break in ages, and I really need one. Don't you think I deserve a little time for myself? You get an extended vacation every year, and no one hassles you. Why are you all up on me like this?"

I wondered if speaking New York street slang was a good idea, but Peter could handle it. We were much more than just business partners, which was what worried me. I sensed that his desperate need for me to come back had little to do with the job and that he wanted something more personal, more intimate, and I wasn't sure I wanted to go down that road.

"Let me tell you what today's been like so far," he started.

"No." I stopped him mid-sentence. "I don't think you're understanding what a vacation is, Peter."

"No, no," he interrupted. "I know what a vacation is, but you're not taking a vacation, you're taking an extended leave. We have no idea when you'll be back, and that scares me, it scares the clients, and it scares the partners."

"Perhaps, but you're all big boys. You can handle it. What did you do before I joined the firm?"

"The firm today is very different from the firm you joined, and most of that is due to you. You brought a unique angle to the business, and no one else can handle your cases like you do."

"But, someone else can handle those cases and, if you give them a chance, they will bring their own unique perspective to their cases that might even be better than mine."

"Well, it's hard to argue with that logic, but I'm afraid we may lose some clients before that happens."

"You're creative, Peter. Surely you're capable of finessing a few clients and keeping on their good side."

The comment silenced him for only a few seconds, and then he suddenly switched gears. "So, what is going on over there in Ireland that I can't get a hold of you? I can't tell you how many times I've called, left emails, and texted you."

"I know, I know. But there are some...'issues'...that have happened here, and I wouldn't feel right leaving until they are resolved."

"That's one of the reasons the firm values you. You know how to deal with the business and put everything else aside. It's just that none of us ever thought that you would find other things so important that you put us aside."

"I always told you, Peter, that life and resources should be equally important. It's never okay to have too much work and too little personal life."

"Well, if it's personal life you want, I can—"

"Forget it, Peter. That's not what I meant, and you know it." I took a pause to gather my thoughts to say what I needed to say clearly. "Listen, I need you to stop calling so often. You know that all these things you're calling me about are completely unnecessary. You just want me to come back to ease your conscience about what you have done. It's not right, and I'm not falling for it. I need this time, and I don't want you constantly bothering me to set your mind at ease. Now, I have some serious matters that must be dealt with here first. When that is done to my satisfaction, I will call you, and then we can talk about when or if I'm coming back."

"*If?* What do you mean, if?"

"We'll talk about that another time. Now, before I hang up, I have another question to ask you."

"Sure, what is it?" His voice suddenly sounded deflated.

"Do we have any international clients here in Ireland?"

"Yes, we do, but are you looking to get into international law?"

"No, it's something personal I'm working on. What bank do they use?"

"Bank? I have no idea. Why would you need to know that?"

"Did you not hear me when I said it was something personal?"

"Oh right."

"Can you find out for me? I'd really appreciate it."

"Sure, I'll do it for you for a favor."

"What kind of favor?"

"I need you to run off a cease and desist order for a client of mine." He hesitated for a brief second. "It's just a compromise." His voice had a teasing lilt to it now. I had bruised his ego, but he had already gotten over it.

We chatted for a few more minutes before we hung up. I had not planned to give in even an inch in the conversation, but, as usual, he had manipulated the conversation to where I had to sacrifice something. It was his strategy all along. He would lead you into thinking that you were in control of the conversation and then flip the script suddenly, and you would end up losing your shirt. This time, I only lost the time to write off one order. I smiled to myself. It was still a good deal.

I hung up the phone and sat there for a minute. I

gazed out over the parking lot and meditated on what I was about to do. A kind of ease had settled over me, and my decision was starting to gel. I had a plan that I hoped was going to make it all easy. I just needed to take care of a few things first.

CHAPTER TWELVE

S tanding outside of the bank's branch office, it was hard to move my feet. After I had taken Mrs. O'Brian back to have lunch with Grams, I finally had some free time to do a little shopping. The plan was to have bought new clothes for myself long before now, but with everything that had happened, it had been nearly impossible. There just had been no time.

But what I was more eager to find out was if I could qualify for a loan here to purchase my own estate and start a new tradition of my own. I had no plan to discuss this with my grams because I just didn't want her to try to sway me one way or another. I knew she would do all she could to keep me here, and I had no objections to that, but I really didn't want her input on how to make that happen.

After I had left the two women back at Gladstone, I was more than eager to take this next step. But, now that I was standing here, I was beginning to have second thoughts. There were butterflies in my stomach, and I thought I would be sick. My biggest fear was that I would be rejected for some reason I hadn't thought of.

My thought was to go back to my computer and do the entire process online, but that was just me chickening out. The personal touch was needed, so I mustered up a little courage and made my way inside.

The air conditioning inside was so cold, I wondered how anyone could stand it. It wasn't that hot outside. In fact, it was a beautiful spring day, and I felt the place could use a few open windows and some fresh air.

"Can I help you?" a young woman asked when she saw me.

"Yes, I'd like to speak to a loan officer, please."

"Certainly," she said in her squeaky clean voice. "If you'll just sign in here and have a seat over there, someone will be with you as soon as they are available."

I gave a curt nod and did as I was told. It was a good thing I brought something to read. In exchange for getting the information on this bank from Peter, he had sent me a case file for the cease and desist order I had agreed to. I spent my time going over the details of the case so I could prepare the order with no discrepancies.

The time went fast. I was barely through reading the first few pages of the case before I heard my name being called.

"Annabelle Shannon."

"Yes," I called out. It was almost like a reflex action. I quickly grabbed my things before following the man into the small glass room.

He gestured to a seat, and took one behind the desk. "I'm Clinton Abbott. It's nice to meet you."

"Nice to meet you, too," I responded politely.

"How can I help you today, Ms. Shannon?"

"I'm thinking of relocating here to Cable Creek, and I thought I would check to see if I could qualify for a loan here in Ireland."

"Hmm. What kind of loan?"

"A mortgage," I told him. "I currently have a home in New York City, and I work for a firm that has close ties to your bank. I have excellent references and excellent credit." I opened a file and laid out my evidence as I spoke.

Mr. Abbott picked up each piece of paper one by one and examined them. "Let's see what we can do." He turned to his computer and began typing on his keyboard. His screen was turned so I couldn't see it, so I could only guess what he was looking for.

"Where do you currently reside?" he asked.

"I'm thinking of relocating here to Cable Creek but right now my only home is in New York."

"Do you have legal residence status here?"

"No. Up until now, I have only visited Ireland, but I love it so much, I'm thinking about moving here."

"It is a wonderful place, isn't it?" He tapped a few more times on the keyboard. "I'm curious. Cable Creek is such a small community, we don't get many outsiders looking to move here. What brings you to our small hamlet?"

"My grandmother lives here. She's been here for generations; maybe you know her? Clarissa Gladstone?"

A broad smile spread across his face. "Who doesn't know Clarissa?" he asked. "You're right, she's a pillar in the community."

I smiled back. Name dropping always works.

He gazed back at the papers I had given him and then back at his keyboard. I was really feeling confident that we were going to work something out, but then he leaned back in his seat and folded his hands over his ample belly.

"You do have excellent credit, and a stellar reputation, Ms. Shannon, but I'm afraid that we won't be able to offer you a loan at this time."

I was stunned. I felt like I had been blindsided by him. "What?" I stammered. "But if you can see…"

"Yes, I can see. You presented an excellent case here, and I can assure you that if I could extend a loan to you, I would. The problem is not that. The problem is that you're not a legal resident of Ireland right now. You don't have anything to connect you to any property you decide to invest in. The bank needs to know that you will be here for the long haul if you want a loan."

I wanted to kick myself. I was a lawyer; I should've known better.

"What can I do?" I asked, feeling more like a school-child than anything else.

"You have several options. First, you could get your grandmother to co-sign for you."

I shook my head. "No, she's getting up in years. I don't want my debt hanging over her head."

"Second, you can obtain a Long Stay 'D' Visa, or get your Irish citizenship. Once you handle any of these conditions, we'll be more than happy to grant you a loan."

By the time I had left the bank, I was completely deflated. I really should've known better. I thought about all the people at the dinner the other night at the Hardcastle. I'm sure if I had been open enough to speak to some of them, I could have been steered in the right direction. Cable Creek is a very small community, and I knew from my grams that the people all worked together. I couldn't afford to be standoffish here like I could in New York. At least, not if I was serious about making this my new home. Anyway, no matter, I knew that these were problems that could easily be fixed; it just may take more time than I had planned.

It was another beautiful spring day, and I needed to lighten my spirits after everything that had happened. Up until this point, nothing had turned out as I had planned, and I was beginning to doubt whether or not Ireland was the paradise I had believed it to be. Everyone was in love with Grams, but the more I tried to blend in, greeting people on the street, giving them my best smile, and trying to be an all-around friendly person, the more I got suspicious stares. It seemed that everyone was a little wary of me, as if they had doubts about whether to accept me or not.

I walked into The Irish Brew, a little coffee shop down the street from the bank. From the outside, it looked like a typical Irish Pub, but the only thing they served was coffee and tea with a few tiny pastries. Feeling a little put out after my visit to the bank, I felt I needed a little pick-me-up. I ordered a coffee and a croissant and settled down at a corner table to catch up on my messages.

Using my tablet, I logged into my email and started gradually going through the gazillion messages I had received over the last few days. Most of them were nothing more than marketing attempts to get me to buy or subscribe to something. I quickly deleted all of those before I began in earnest to look at the more serious messages.

I was so engrossed in my task that I barely heard the voice of the man at the table next to mine.

"Excuse me," he said.

I blinked a couple of times to bring myself back to the present moment and looked up to see a tall, thin man who appeared to be in his early thirties.

"Yes?" I said, wondering who he was. "Can I help you?" I couldn't for the life of me figure out what he wanted. I glanced down at my table to see if there were any salt and pepper shakers he may have needed to borrow, but there was nothing.

"Are you Annabelle Shannon?"

I stared at him. "Yes, I am. How did you know?" I asked, suddenly feeling like I was being investigated.

Without an invitation, he pulled up a chair and sat across from me. "My name is Colin Murphy. I am new in Cable Creek, too." He coughed slightly before he continued, "I know you're not from around here either, so I thought that maybe I could ask you a few questions."

I sat up straighter in my chair—he had piqued my curiosity.

"I would ask you to have a seat, but you've already done that." I tipped my head in his direction and gestured toward the seat he was now occupying.

"Oh, I'm sorry about that. I guess I tend to be impulsive sometimes." He gave a slight chuckle and then turned serious again.

"So, how do you know my name, and what do you think I can tell you? I'm new in this area myself."

"That's why I wanted to talk to you. From what I hear, you just arrived here in Cable Creek a few days ago, but I've already seen you have connected with a lot of people here. It seems that when I talk to people, they are very cautious of me. I know this is a small community but I love it so much, I would like to make my home here."

His words struck a chord with me. I knew exactly what he was talking about. "I understand what you mean, Colin. The thing is, I don't know if I could have broken through the social wall myself, if my grams hadn't been here to smooth the way for me."

"So, that little old lady I saw you with was your grandmother?"

I laughed a little. "You're in Cable Creek now. Almost every woman you meet will be a little old lady. I've spent quite a bit of time with several old ladies since I've been here; it depends on which one you saw me with."

"Oh, yeah. I was talking about the woman whose husband died. I saw you at the hotel that night, and I saw you with her again this morning."

A sense of concern began to come over me. This man knew every place I had been, and who I had been with. I leaned forward and stared at him closely, but his face didn't seem familiar to me at all.

"How do you know all of this about me?" I asked, my guard coming up.

He put his hands out defensively, like he was trying to stop a truck. "Oh, don't worry," he said. "I'm not following you or anything. It's just that in a small town like Cable Creek, it's pretty easy for outsiders to stand out. I was in the bank when you came in this morning."

"I'm sorry," I said. "I didn't notice you."

"I was in the room next to yours. I wanted to get a loan so I could buy some property around here."

"Me too," I told him, starting to feel a kindred spirit developing between us. "Unfortunately, they told me no."

"Me too," he said. "But I'm glad I'm not the only one that was rejected." He dropped his gaze down to the table before he spoke again. "So, do you have a property in mind that you want to buy?"

I took a sip of my coffee before I answered. "No, not

yet. I just wanted to see if I would qualify for a loan before I started looking."

I thought I saw a flash of relief in his eyes before he continued. "I started looking first and there are a few properties that are prime for development. I just want to get my hands on them."

"Development?!" I was surprised. "What do you mean by development?"

"I would like to put in a residential community so more people could afford to live here."

"But the people here take a lot of pride in the history of this town. A modern development would destroy that image." I took a calming breath before I spoke again. I didn't want to jump to any more conclusions. "I thought you said you wanted to live here."

He smiled in a way I had seen a thousand times before. It was the smile of a corporate bureaucrat that believed that no one could touch him, and his attempts to make money superseded anything else.

At that moment, I felt a twinge of dislike bubbling up inside of me, but I didn't let it show.

"Well, I'm not sure I understand what you want from me," I said. "It seems that you already know more than I do about the place."

"I guess I should get to the point." He waited a moment to make sure he had my full attention. "I know that Mr. O'Brian's death has come to a shock to everyone in this town. I had already been talking to him about buying his property for my new development. I was hoping that you could talk to Mrs. O'Brian about closing the deal that her husband started. Now that her husband is gone, I doubt she'll have the ability to manage that property all on her own."

I couldn't hide the shock on my face. "I'm sorry, but her husband just died."

"I understand that, but I'm on a very strict timetable. You look like you're a pretty astute businesswoman; you must understand the deadlines in this type of business."

I glared at him, incredulous at his insensitivity.

"First," I began, "I don't know the O'Brians that well. I just met them that night at the hotel so I don't know that I have as much influence as you think. In addition, from what I know about the O'Brians and most of the property owners in Cable Creek is that you're not likely to find any buyers for your development."

He looked a bit disappointed but he brushed it off. "I'm not asking you to do anything. Just get me in the room with Mrs. O'Brian, and I can take care of the rest."

"Your determination is astounding. I can't believe you would ask me to do this."

"Personally, I think you have more influence than

you admit, and I'm pretty confident that you can make this meeting happen."

He stood up from his chair, reached in his pocket, and pulled out a business card. "I'll make it worth your while," he said casually. He dropped the card on the table and walked out.

My eyes followed him all the way to the door. No question, he was a bold one, but there was no reason for me to take his words seriously. Just a greedy corporate exec who thought his money had all the power in the world.

I looked at his card and wondered what kind of man would force his own interests over the unstable emotions of a grieving widow, or if he was just one to use her grief to get what he wanted. I crinkled up my nose at the gaudy logo he had chosen. I hadn't been here long but I didn't see any Cable Creek quality in him. Besides, who puts their photograph on a business card in this type of community? My first instinct was to toss the card in the trash, but instead, I slipped it into my pocket and went back to my emails.

I was at it for another few minutes before my phone sprung to life again. I checked the caller ID and groaned. It was Peter again.

"Yes, Peter," I said when I answered. "I have already

done your cease and desist order and will send it to you in the morning."

"I know. I appreciate that."

"You know, that was an easy document to do. You were more than capable of doing it yourself."

"I know, I know. It's just my way of making sure that your fingers are still in the pot with the rest of us."

"Are you that worried, Peter?"

"I hate to admit it, but yes. I'm resorting to all sorts of trickery to get you to remember your place in this firm."

I smiled a little bit. As irritating as Peter could be, I knew his heart was in the right place.

"You don't have to do that, Peter. I keep telling you that I need some time to sort things out."

"That's what I'm afraid of. You're one of the best lawyers our firm has ever had. We don't want to lose you."

"You have plenty of capable lawyers in your firm."

"This I know, but your approach to the cases is unique. You have a no-frills attack method on each case, and you go in with a full-on 'take no prisoners' attitude every time."

"Peter, you have to admit that while that approach is successful, it can take its toll."

"Trust me, I have had my fair share of ups and downs, too. Being a lawyer is no easy job, and dealing with corporate temperaments is no help. I've been there, done that. I just want you to know that we need you back here."

I started to speak again but he cut me off.

"And to make sure that you do come back, we are prepared to offer you a full partnership in the company, no strings attached."

"What about money?" It just slipped out. I had been doing business negotiations for so long, the conversation had become second nature to me.

"I'm pretty sure we can come to a mutually beneficial agreement, when you get back here."

There was a flirtatious air to the last comment. If Peter was anything, he was determined, and it was going to be hard to say no to him, but I was not going to let that influence my decision in any way.

"Well, as I promised you before, I'll give it some thought, but don't expect an answer right away. I still need time to think."

When the conversation was over, I knew I had a lot to think about. I just wasn't sure if I wanted to go back into that life. New York was fast-paced, expensive, and sometimes just plain old out of control. I finished my coffee and decided to take a walk, so I could enjoy some of Cable Creek's beautiful landscape.

CHAPTER THIRTEEN

*E*verywhere I looked, there was some of Ireland's natural beauty. The lush green hills and valleys were breathtaking. In the park, I stopped and scooped up a handful of the dark, rich soil that guaranteed a colorful spring and summer every year. Visions of me and my father, planting trees and frolicking in the Irish sunshine, floated through my mind. Maybe I could still fulfill his dream of creating a fresh, organic farm to service this aging community. It would be a very different lifestyle from the one I had now, and the more I thought of him, the more I wanted to make his dream come true.

The memories were followed by sadness though. I missed him so much every day and wondered if I would ever see him again. Wc had been so close, losing him had felt like I had lost a part of me when it had happened. I couldn't believe that all these years later, I still felt the pain of his absence.

I shook my head to get back in focus. *Shake it off*, I told myself. *Shake it off. There's nothing I can do about that, but there's something I can do to remember him.* Then my thoughts drifted to Peter. Definitely a flirtatious man and not accustomed to any women, including me, putting him on the back burner. He was going to be a problem, and I had to figure out a way to handle him. It was going to be difficult, considering his reputation. Already divorced three times, I knew that a trip down that road was unlikely to yield any type of positive results. He was a man that was used to getting what he wanted, and I'm not so naive as to think that all of the calls he was making were purely for business purposes. It would have been better if it was for business, but I knew better than that.

I finally made my way to the quaint little street that served as a shopping center for the town. There were clothing, jewelry, and shoe stores along a tree-lined street that appeared to be a throwback from the fifties. It was either that or they never left that era in the first place.

I tried to bury myself in my favorite pastime, but the thoughts of the O'Brians kept popping into my head, and then those thoughts were followed by a whole stream of ideas, suppositions, and conclusions that I kept ruminating on. It was almost impossible to keep my focus, and I found I wasn't getting the joy that I thought I would have.

I finally settled on a varied selection of clothes, shoes, and accessories that would help me fit in better, and I headed back to the car. It had been a rather unfruitful morning, and it didn't promise to get any better.

The drive back to Gladstone was uneventful, so I lulled myself into believing that the rest of the day would be equally uneventful. But thoughts of Colin and his insensitivity started to make me feel angry again. So, I deliberately tried to redirect my thoughts to someone else. I had to remind myself that the police had yet to rule on whether or not it was a homicide, so until they did, there was little anyone could do about pushing the case forward. So, for the time being, I would just have to put it out of my mind.

That idea didn't last long. As I drove up the drive to Gladstone, I saw a single police car, its lights flashing, parked at the bottom of the steps. My heart skipped a beat as I wondered about all the possibilities. What could have happened while I was gone? I quickly pulled the car into Grams' garage and jumped out, running as fast as I could up the steps.

I took them two at a time, so I was already feeling winded when I reached the door. I paused only for a second to catch my breath and let my eyes scan the room to assess the situation. Instead of them collected in Grams' parlor where she usually entertained guests, I found them gathered in the massive great room in the front. There, gathered in front of the old fireplace, I found a uniformed police officer, Mrs. O'Brian, Grams, and Liam. If I didn't already have my suspicions, I would have found the scene to be quite cozy, but the looks on their faces made me wonder what had happened since I'd left just a few hours before.

"Oh, Belle," Grams nearly shouted my name as I joined them. "I'm so glad you're back. There has been a development, and you need to hear this."

"A development?" I asked. "What kind of development?" My eyes went straight to the officer for the answer.

"I'm Detective O'Malley. I've been assigned to the O'Brian case."

"So, what happened?" I asked again.

He was leaning up against the mantle with his hands deep in his pockets and his ankles crossed. When he moved, his hands stayed buried deep inside, causing him to walk with a strange kind of gait.

"We got the preliminary reports from the coroner this morning."

"That was fast."

"It's unprecedented, for sure," he agreed, but he didn't seem to enjoy saying that. "It seems that your deductions were correct, Annabelle. While it is not being ruled as a homicide just yet, the case has been marked as suspicious. We need to do further investigation to determine what really happened in that hotel room."

"So, they're saying it wasn't a heart attack?"

"The preliminary results do not support that conclusion." He pulled out one hand from his pockets and scratched behind his ear. "Needless to say, if it does turn out to be a homicide, everyone who was in the Hardcastle that night becomes a suspect, including you."

"What on earth for?" I asked even though I knew he was right. If it was a homicide, then all of us would have to be investigated.

"Because you were all together and would have had some contact with Mr. O'Brian during the course of the evening before. We'll have to interview everyone."

"What about the cause of death? If it wasn't a heart attack, then what was it?"

"That is the question of the day, Ms. Shannon. So, now that we are all here, I believe we need to get started eliminating each of you from our list of potential suspects."

I took a seat in a large armchair that sat in front of the fireplace. "I think that's a good and sensible idea. Shoot."

O'Malley looked up at me and almost laughed. "No, I think I should interview each of you separately. It's easier to find inconsistencies in your stories when you are not together." He looked around the room at each of us. "I think I'll start with you," he said, pointing to Grams.

He followed Grams into the dining room, leaving Mrs. O'Brian, Liam, and me alone. I wanted to object to the whole scenario, but I couldn't. I knew that for now he was just doing his job, and because there was no investigation when all the guests were in one place, he was already behind the eight ball. I wondered if he would ever catch up.

Once they disappeared from sight, I tried to strain my ears to see if I could hear anything, but in this drafty old place, I couldn't hear anything from outside the massive dining hall. Glancing over at Mrs. O'Brian, I couldn't help but notice that she was sitting there rubbing her arms up and down as if she had just come out of the cold.

"Lillian, are you cold?" I asked her. "Would you like for me to build a fire for you in the fireplace?"

"No, don't be silly, child. I guess I'm still in a little bit of shock."

"I suppose you're right," I told her. Then I got up from my seat and walked over to the fireplace to stand in the same position O'Malley had been only moments earlier.

"Lillian," I started. "How long has he been here?"

She looked up, casting her eyes at Liam, who had yet to say anything. "Who?"

"The police officer."

She shrugged her shoulders. "I don't know. Maybe fifteen…twenty minutes."

I nodded my head, but I was feeling uncomfortable about the whole situation. "Did he say anything when he came?"

"No, nothing. He just asked if he could come in and told us he asked Liam to come here so he could talk to all of us together."

"He's fishing for something," I mumbled out loud. "He has his own suspicions, but he's not saying just yet."

"Is this a bad thing?" she asked.

"Maybe, maybe not. I won't know until I get a chance

to talk to him." I looked around the great room. There was only Mrs. O'Brian and myself there. "Where did Liam go?"

"I don't know. He was just here a minute ago."

I stepped out into the foyer to see if he had gone there, but he wasn't anywhere in the immediate vicinity. He had been unusually quiet, and then just disappeared. "I wonder where he went…" I said, returning to the great room.

"He can't be far. Maybe he just went to the bathroom," she said, rubbing her hands together.

"Yeah, maybe."

We sat in silence for about twenty minutes. I spent my time looking around the room. I hadn't noticed before, but there was a large collection of flowers and cards set along one wall. Apparently, everyone in Cable Creek had sent something to Mrs. O'Brian to offer their condolences. I only wished I had that kind of respect when my time came.

"Nice flowers," I said to her, but she only grunted in answer. I was pretty sure that it was going to be another difficult day, and I vowed to stay close in case she needed me. About a half an hour later, O'Malley and Grams returned to the great room. To my amusement, Grams didn't appear to be agitated or upset in any way. In fact, she was smiling. But O'Malley, on the other hand, looked like he had just been put through the wringer. I chuckled a little to myself as I observed his nervous tic.

"Where's Liam?" he asked as he scanned the room.

"Don't know," I answered honestly.

He looked in my direction and appeared to be analyzing me.

I returned the look and added a little defiance to his, then hunched up my shoulders. "Honest. He just walked out without saying a word. I have no idea where he went."

O'Malley pulled out his radio and walked out into the foyer to say something. When he returned, he just pointed to me and said, "You're next."

I was about to follow him into the dining room, but then I heard a small, little yelp from Mrs. O'Brian. I looked back to see if everything was okay. She was sitting in her chair, vigorously rubbing her arms as if she was freezing.

"Lillian," I started. "I can make you a fire if you're cold."

"Maybe you should," she said. "I have such a chill, it feels like something crawling all over my skin."

"Maybe it's just a combination of shock and exhaustion," Grams told her. "Why don't we take you up to your room where you can rest. It's been a difficult few days that you've had to go through."

She nodded her agreement and the two older women started down the back hall together, chatting about anything that came into their minds.

"What if I need to talk to them again?" O'Malley asked, trying to decide if he should object.

"Don't be such a power-tripper. They are two little old ladies; where are they going to go?" I asked before heading into the dining room. "Have a seat," I told him, letting him know that he was not in charge.

He paused and stared at me before slipping into a seat at the table.

He put his elbows on the table and gently massaged his eyes. "I think we got off on the wrong foot."

"You think?" Once I let the words leave my mouth, I began to feel a little guilty. The man was only doing what he was trained to do, and if this turned out to be a murder, which I suspected it was, it was not a common thing for them to deal with. Of course they would make mistakes.

"I'm sorry," I told him. "I guess I'm a little edgy right now."

"Don't worry about it. I get it. You're here on vacation, and now you're a suspect in a possible homicide. I would be a little testy, too."

"So, you are leaning towards homicide?"

"Nothing is definite yet, but we know it wasn't a heart attack. The coroner is only listing it as suspicious now."

"You said that, but you wouldn't be here questioning little old ladies if you had even the slightest clue of what happened?"

"It's still in the preliminary stages." He pulled out his pen and pad and made a note in his little book. "Now, how well did you know the O'Brians?" he asked.

"I didn't. I just met them."

"What about your grandmother?"

"They grew up together. They've probably been friends for fifty, maybe sixty years."

"I watched you with her—Mrs. O'Brian. You seemed to be very comfortable with her."

"I suppose so. My grams loves them very much, so protecting and taking care of them would be the same as taking care of her. They are dear to her so they are dear to me."

"But by your own admission, you'd just met."

"That's right, but because my grams cares so much about them, protecting them is the same as protecting her."

"Did your grams say anything to you about the O'Brians' business dealings?"

"I don't think so. I'm not sure that she knew anything

about it. In fact, I don't think even Lillian knew anything about it."

"Why would you say that?" The pen he was scribbling with stopped in the middle of a word. From where I sat, I couldn't see what he was writing, but I had struck a nerve and he had reacted. "Do you have any idea why anyone would want to hurt Mr. O'Brian?"

"Can't think of any. Didn't know what or even if he was into anything."

He glanced up at me and stared as if he was trying to decide if I was telling the truth. I let the silence hang in the air, and I could tell it was making him a little fidgety. This was not going the way he had planned. I had seized control of the conversation, and he couldn't figure out how to get it back.

"When did you arrive in Cable Creek?"

"Two days ago. I'm from New York City."

"How long do you plan to stay here?"

"I don't know. A few weeks, maybe longer."

"From my understanding, it could be longer than that. I'm sorry to hear that you won't be getting the loan from the bank to buy your own piece of land."

For once, I was speechless. I was getting tired of people talking about me. "How did you find out about that?"

"We have one of our agents in the bank, right now;

working on another case, of course. In fact, he's been working for us for quite some time."

"Why?" Was Cable Creek a hotbed of criminal activity that I didn't know anything about? "As you already know, I'm not from around here, but my guess is that eavesdropping on people's personal affairs borders on invasion of privacy."

He chuckled a little. "Don't worry. We don't have any of your personal information, and we won't share it, unless we deem you as a real suspect."

"That's a relief. What would that take?"

"The only reason you're not a serious suspect now is because you haven't any motive that we know of."

"Um. That's a relief. Who does have a motive?"

"I'm sorry, we're not ready to share that information just yet. Now back to my question about your grand-mother. Do you think they got along well, she and the O'Brians?"

"As far as I can tell. She never mentioned them to me before that night. I don't know anything about their history. Are you thinking she may be a suspect?"

"Anything's possible, but not right now, no."

Frustrated, I decided to lay all my cards on the table. "Listen. If you knew me, you'd learn that I'm on your side. I'm really good at figuring stuff out. If you'd let me, I could be of real help to you."

"Maybe, but you don't have any police background. You might get into trouble and cause more problems for us."

I was about to respond when the door burst open, and Charlotte came running in. "Annabelle! Annabelle!" she screamed in a near panic.

"What? What is it?"

"It's Mrs. O'Brian. There's something wrong with her."

CHAPTER FOURTEEN

My jaw dropped slightly at what Charlotte had just told us. "Something wrong with Mrs. O'Brian? I just left her; she was fine."

"I don't know what happened," Charlotte said. "She was just sitting there one minute and then she started stamping her feet and crying out. I think she's very sick. We have to get her to a hospital."

I jumped to my feet and ran the full length of the hallway back to Grams' parlor where I found Grams trying to kneel her old body over the convulsing figure of her friend.

"What is it? What happened?" I asked as I dropped down on the floor beside her.

"I don't know."

Spencer was on his knees trying to hold the woman

in a stable position. He seemed to have no idea what he was doing, or if it would work, but Mrs. O'Brian was still contorting and seizing while crying out in pain at the same time.

"Spencer!" Grams shouted. "Go get the car. We have to get her to the hospital now!"

Spencer jumped up, turned on his heels, and fled out the door without another word.

"Charlotte!"

"Yes, ma'am." The young girl was just a step away from hysteria.

"Run to my room and grab some pillows and blankets and bring them here as fast as you can."

Charlotte took off running.

"We should call paramedics," O'Malley said, speaking into his radio.

"No. There's no time!" Grams shouted at him. "We need to get her to the hospital now."

Charlotte returned with the pillow and blankets and in a matter of seconds, Mrs. O'Brian was wrapped in a blanket, and Spencer was carrying her out the door to the car with O'Malley right behind him.

The hospital waiting room was quiet. My mind was racing, and I didn't know how to sort out my thoughts. I was fighting hard to slow my heart rate down but it seemed to have a mind of its own. From what I had just seen, it looked like the same thing that had happened to Mr. O'Brian, but he had been all alone, and there was no one there to help him.

I glanced over at Officer O'Malley and wondered what he was thinking. Did this put my grams in his sights, or could it be Liam, who had mysteriously disappeared and hadn't shown up again? Where was he, and why did he leave so abruptly? It seemed that as soon as he heard we were all going to be questioned, he just slipped out and was nowhere to be found.

They had taken Mrs. O'Brian straight away, and we had heard nothing since. I glanced over at Grams, who looked like she was in shock. Spencer was sitting there with Charlotte's head in his lap. The poor girl had been so traumatized that she couldn't take it anymore and had just fallen asleep, completely exhausted. It was just by sheer luck that they had come to visit when they did.

"Does anyone want some coffee?" I offered, getting up from my seat. I was feeling antsy and didn't want to sit still anymore. I needed to move around. Needed to do something.

No one answered me. I wasn't even sure if they had

heard me. I decided to just bring some for everyone anyway.

The nurse directed me down another hall to the cafeteria, and I headed that way, trying to find ways to make sense of it all. Deep in thought, I automatically picked up a tray and started to fill it with rolls, breads, and treats. I figured I would just get a little of everything, so they could pick and choose what they wanted.

I was so deep in thought that I was completely surprised when I heard O'Malley's voice behind me.

"Quite an afternoon, huh?" he asked.

"Yes, it was," I agreed. "Still think Mr. O'Brian had a heart attack?" I didn't even try to hide the sarcasm in my voice.

"No, I have to admit, this is too much of a coincidence. It's obvious that someone wanted the O'Brians out of the way."

"That's an understatement. But the question is how, and why?"

"Listen, I'm not a detective like they have in the big city, so help me out here. What are you thinking?"

I moved down the cafeteria line behind another gentleman who was examining an assortment of fruit cups and trying to decide which one he wanted.

"Well, I've got the feeling that once we find out what caused Mrs. O'Brian's seizure, we can backtrack a trail to who killed Mr. O'Brian. We also need to figure out the motive. From what I know, everyone who knew them had great affection for them. They are like my grams—no one had any reason to harm them. They weren't in business, they owned their property outright, they weren't in debt, and they had no other interests that we know of. They were just two retired people trying to live out their final years in peace. Still, someone did this to them, and once we find out the how and why, we can find the who."

CHAPTER FIFTEEN

I paid for the tray of food I had collected, O'Malley took care of the coffee, and we both walked back to the waiting room. Grams quickly grabbed a croissant and a cup of coffee, but I could tell she would have rather had tea.

We all sat together to discuss what had happened. Suddenly, O'Malley wasn't so suspicious of us anymore.

"I just don't get it," Grams was saying. "Who would do something like this?"

"Grams, you know them better than anyone. Who do you think would do it?"

"I can't fathom. They were the salt of the earth and as far as I knew, everyone loved them."

"Perhaps you're thinking about this the wrong way," O'Malley put in. "Instead of trying to figure out the who, let's try to list the reasons why someone might have wanted to harm them."

I tapped him on his shoulder. "But first, let's see if we know the how." I nodded my head in the direction of the door where two of the doctors had just entered.

Grams seemed anxious to get on her feet, but she just couldn't move as fast as she wanted to. I had to help her.

"Did you find out anything?" O'Malley asked. "How is she doing?"

"Do you know her next of kin?" one of the doctors asked.

"She doesn't have any family here. We're her family," Grams said indignantly.

"I see."

The two doctors conferred with each other before turning back to us.

"Why don't you follow us," one of them said.

He turned and led us through the emergency doors and took us to a small private room where he invited us to sit.

Grams seemed to be growing impatient. "Tell us, will you?" she snapped.

"The good news is that you got her here in time. She had absorbed a powerful toxin that caused the convulsions."

"A toxin?"

"Yes, it's called aconite. It grows in many of the flowers found around here, but no one eats them, so I'm guessing she consumed them topically."

"Topically?"

"Yeah, that means through the skin."

My mind immediately went to the assortment of flowers that had been delivered today.

"Lillian wouldn't have done anything like that," Grams said. "She grew up around here, and she knows more about the plant life here than anybody I know."

"Well then, you have a problem. You have to find out how this toxin got into her system."

"Is she going to be okay?"

"We don't know. There's no real treatment for aconite poisoning."

I shuddered when I heard the word. It made the whole thing sound so deliberate.

O'Malley spoke up, "Her husband died just a day ago, and I think he may have been exposed to the same toxin. What are the symptoms?"

One of the doctors reared back in his chair and pressed the tips of his fingers together as he collected his thoughts. "We're dealing with what is called a cardiotoxin and a neurotoxin. When exposed to it, it interferes with the body's ability to communicate between the heart and the nervous system. The resulting symptoms could be acute abdominal pain, nausea, seizures, and a tingling sensation on the skin. Some people claim it feels like something is crawling over them. It can also slow down the heartbeat, and until it passes through the system, she may have difficulty breathing."

"Oh my," Grams gasped.

"There is no treatment we can give her, but she's in a good place now. As long as we monitor her closely, we can immediately counteract any of the negative effects of the toxin with treatments right here, and she has a good chance of pulling through."

"But, doctor, she's seventy years old."

"And that is working against her now, but if she has any chance of beating this, it will be because she's here where we can stay on top of any negative reactions. This will give her a fighting chance."

"Doctor," I said. "What about the person that gave her the toxin? Wouldn't they have symptoms, too?"

"That depends on how they handled it. If they know they had the potential of exposure, they may have worn protective covering. Because it can slow down the breathing, and if they inhaled any of it, even just a tiny amount, they will likely walk around with a telling cough for a few days."

"So, when will we know if she is going to pull

through?" O'Malley asked.

"Tonight is going to be the toughest. I'd say if she makes it through the night, she'll have a good chance at a full recovery."

We left the hospital, stunned by the whole situation. We all drove back to Gladstone in silence. What was there to say? We needed to find out who did this, and we needed to do it soon.

O'Malley followed us back in his squad car and offered to take Spencer and Charlotte home. It was already dark out, and the roads were not safe enough for them to walk.

"Listen," he said to me as Grams and I were heading up the steps. "Let's get together tomorrow and try to trace back this problem. I'm going to update the sergeant on what happened here tonight, but right now, I don't know what to think."

I was surprised at his change of attitude. He had come down quite a bit from his pedestal. It was hard to believe it was the same person.

"Do you still think we could be prime suspects?" I asked.

"I never said you were prime suspects, just that

everyone in the hotel was a suspect."

"Potato, potahto."

"Fine." He smiled at me. "See it your way. I'll stop by and check on you in the morning."

"Fine, but not too early. Grams needs her rest, and so do I."

"I'll call first."

After I made sure Grams was in bed, I climbed the stairs to my room. My mind was full of thoughts, and I knew that sleep was going to elude me. I had to sort all of this out if I ever hoped to sleep again, especially since the O'Brians were so close to Grams. I feared that what had happened to them would one day happen to her as well. I needed to work this out now.

I stayed up the better part of the night, trying to put the pieces together. Opening up my computer, I tried to do a little research on aconite. Where did it come from? How was it processed? How would someone get it into their system? The whole thing was very confusing. Then I started thinking about the dinner. O'Malley was right —if Mr. O'Brian had received aconite poisoning, it would have been from someone at the hotel, but I couldn't think of anyone I had met that night that had a reason for killing him. Everyone was so happy to see the O'Brians, and there had been no suspicious behavior observed with any of them.

By the time dawn came around, I had still not gone to sleep. As soon as I thought it was a reasonable hour, I gave O'Malley a call.

"What have you found out?" I asked him.

"Not much, I'm afraid. How about you?"

"Same here, but I think I know how to flush the killer out."

"What? Are you trying to play detective again?"

"Maybe, but you have to admit, I am doing much better at this than you."

There was a hesitancy on the other end, and I was afraid his masculinity was once again going to get the better of him.

"All right, what are you thinking?" he asked with a yawn.

"I'm thinking we all need to go back to the Hardcastle tonight."

"For what?"

"A reenactment."

"I don't know."

"It'll be fine. We need to redo the entire evening, and I'm sure the truth will come out."

O'Malley didn't seem convinced but he semi-agreed.

"Let me run it by the sergeant, and I'll get back to you."

He hung up, and my thoughts now went to Liam. He had disappeared yesterday, and I still had no idea what had happened to him. I was beginning to wonder if he had been behind it all. He certainly had access to the room, the food, the dining room, and every other corner of the hotel. If anyone had an opportunity, it would have been him, but for the life of me, I couldn't think of any reason he would want to have them killed. He had a fine hotel and restaurant, a successful business with no ties to the O'Brians, and as far as anyone knew, he had no secrets that had been uncovered. As a matter of fact, the death could cast a dark shadow on his hotel's reputation, and he wouldn't want that.

Then I thought about Officer Hanlon. Here was someone who was reluctant to investigate the case himself. Why did he fight me so hard on it? And why had he been so resistant? I found it hard to believe that he was so inept that he would botch a police investigation and mess everything up. It would put his career and reputation at risk, and for what? What was his motive? Could he have been protecting someone else? If so, from what?

Even though I had not been to sleep, I got dressed and went down to talk to Grams. If we could chat together, maybe we could pick up on something that may have been overlooked.

CHAPTER SIXTEEN

$\mathcal{I}$t was quite an event to prepare for the second showing at the Hardcastle, especially since we had to clear everything through Liam. He never came back to Gladstone, so I couldn't talk to him. All I knew was that O'Malley was able to track him down, but he failed to give a reasonable answer for why he had left so abruptly. However, he was more than willing to help us to flush out the killer.

In addition to all the guests being present, it was also necessary for all of the staff to be the same. The killer could have been anyone in the hotel that night, and since no one could come up with a possible motive for the murder, the staff could not be excluded.

We entered into that grand entryway that had so impressed me that first day, but this time I didn't feel so mesmerized. Liam greeted us in the same way, and the same worker took us up to our room to wait until the rest of the guests had arrived.

Grams and I were in the same room as before, and the only person who I knew for a fact was not going to be there was Mrs. O'Brian, since she was still in the hospital recovering from her ordeal. Grams was so relieved to find she was getting better and would soon be able to go home. Still, I wasn't quite sure that was a blessing for her. Someone had already killed her husband and had also made an attempt on her life. If we didn't catch the killer tonight, there was no way we were going to let her return home alone.

At the appointed time, the knock came, and we were escorted downstairs to the dining room. I was impressed. Between O'Malley and Liam, they had thought of every detail. The room looked exactly the same—even the menu was identical. It was an amazing feat to complete to such perfection on such short notice.

In the dining room, everyone was scattered around the large room, whispering among each other. The tone of the conversations were different throughout. Before, we all praised the amazing designs and decor. We had admired the nice balance between the history of the place and the subtle changes over time. This time though, the conversation was much more subdued. Everyone here watched each other carefully through eyes of suspicion. I felt the atmosphere of Cable Creek had suddenly shifted. Before there was a community of people who loved to work and play together, but now, there was a powerful spirit of distrust that hung heavy in that room.

We all took our usual seats at the table, and then O'Malley, the only one who wasn't there from before, spoke to everyone.

"Listen, everyone," he said. "I know this is going to be a very uncomfortable evening tonight, and I can assure you, we're going to make it as painless as possible. The reason we called you all here tonight is to try to determine what happened to Mr. O'Brian. We need to stage out the events of the evening, so if you all could do the same as you did the night before his demise, it will help the entire evening to go faster."

"I don't understand why we are doing this tonight?" said one woman at the other end of the table. "I mean, he died the next morning, not that night."

"I know, but we're examining all interactions with anyone who had contact with him."

"But why?"

"Because we don't know when or how he was assaulted."

"He was assaulted?" said another woman. "I just thought he had a heart attack."

"If it was a heart attack then we wouldn't need to be here, would we?"

"Well, how do you know if everyone is playing their part the same as before?"

"That's why we asked all of you to come in at the same time. You'll each check each other. If someone does something different, the others here will notice."

The group burst into a lot of murmuring, making it clear that none of them wanted to be there. It was one thing to be invited as a free guest to a premier of a new hotel and another thing entirely to be asked by the police to flush out a killer.

"People, people, can you please calm down?"

The murmuring settled down, but only slightly.

"Do you think this is gonna work?" Grams asked.

I nodded my head, but I was beginning to have my doubts. No one there seemed to have any idea what was going to happen, and everyone was clearly nervous.

We all took our seats and started with the usual chatter. O'Malley sat next to Grams where Mr. and Mrs. O'Brian had been sitting. In the beginning, everything went smoothly. Surprisingly, O'Malley and I fell into an easy and comfortable chat, while the staff went about doing their duties the same as they had before. Nothing seemed to be out of the ordinary. We had reached a point where we were about to give up and send everyone to their rooms. But then one detail hit me.

"Wait a minute," I almost shouted when I realized what was missing.

"What?" O'Malley asked, and everyone in the room turned in my direction.

"Mr. O'Brian jumped up about this time."

"That's right," Grams said. "He jumped out of his seat in a panic."

O'Malley looked confused. "Why?"

"He said that bugs had run across his foot."

Grams nodded. "We all got up to look for them."

"Yes," Liam agreed. "It put an end to the dinner."

There was a consensus of agreement all around the room.

"But what has that got to do with anything?" O'Malley asked.

"Everything," I said with a proud grin. "Everything." I sat there for a moment trying to collect my thoughts. "I did some research on aconite poisoning, and I discovered something interesting that confirms what one of the doctors had told us. One of the symptoms of aconite toxicity is the feeling that something is crawling on your skin. We all thought his neuropathy was acting up, but he must have received the toxin before that happened."

"So his exposure must've happened in this room, during dinner or maybe just before."

"But we still don't know who slipped it to him."

"We know it had to be someone in this room, but we have to narrow it down to something more specific."

"What about the strange man?" Grams said.

"What strange man?" Liam asked.

"You know, the one who came in right before everything happened. You know him, Liam, because he came in and stood at the door and beckoned you from across the room. He was an older gentleman, wearing a suit, and he looked very stern. You were talking to us and then you went out with him."

"Oh yeah. No, he didn't have anything to do with it. He was just my uncle who came down to have me sign some business papers for the family."

"It couldn't have been him anyway," I added. "It had to be someone here at this end of the table. Up until he had jumped out of his seat, everyone had stayed in their seats, so no one else could have slipped him the toxin. Just before his panic, who was here at this end of the table?"

"No one," Grams said. "It was just me, you, Georgina sat across from us, and the O'Brians."

"No, there was one other person. A waiter," I said.

"A waiter?" Liam asked, his face turning a little white.

"Yes. I remember he came and poured our drinks for us and left." I turned to Grams. "You talked to him, and you were all laughing. I heard you but I was talking to another guy…his name was…it was…David, I think. A few minutes after he poured our drinks, Mr. O'Brian jumped out of his seat."

"All right," Liam said, sounding skeptical. "Let me get the waiters to come out and pour the drinks." He excused himself, and a few minutes later, the waitstaff all appeared, carrying large pitchers of water for everyone.

The one who approached to pour our drinks was a young man, maybe in his early twenties, with a little ponytail tied in the back of his head. He leaned down to pour, but Grams stopped him.

"No, not you," she said.

The young man looked confused. "Excuse me?"

"You're not the one who poured our drinks that night."

I took a closer look at him, not quite sure she was right.

"He's not the one?" I asked.

Liam came over to check. "Oscar, were you working here that night?"

Oscar looked a little frightened. Red spread up his

neck and his cheeks like a red tide that overtook him. "No, sir," he said quietly.

Liam looked angry. "I thought I made it clear that only those who had worked the other night were to report to work today." He looked around at his other workers. "Did anyone else come here that wasn't supposed to?"

No one responded.

"Who was here?" he asked, turning his attention back to Oscar.

"It was the new kid."

"What new kid? You're all new!"

"I mean he was the one who came in that night. He said you hired him at the last minute."

"I didn't hire anybody else. Do you know who he was?"

"No, sir."

"Do you know what he looked like?"

"Yes, sir. He was a little older than me. Maybe in his thirties, late thirties. Kinda slim, you know. An average kind of guy."

"Wait a minute," I said. "I think I know who it was. Would you recognize him if I showed you a picture?"

"I think so."

"I would, too," Grams added.

"I'm sure of it now," I said. "And if it is who I think it is, I can give you a motive, too."

"How can you do that?" Liam asked.

I picked up my bag and fished around for what I was looking for. When I found it, I handed it to Oscar. "Is that him?"

Oscar gazed at the photo on the business card and immediately responded, "Yes, yes that's him," and handed it back to me. I handed it to Grams.

"That's him," she agreed.

"That's the man that was at Gladstone yesterday," Liam added.

I turned to Liam. "What? He was at Gladstone? For what?"

"He said he wanted to see Mrs. O'Brian." He looked at me. "You were in the dining room with Officer O'Malley, and Grams was in the kitchen, fixing some tea. I was outside on a phone call, and he said he had flowers for her." There was a look of panic on his face. "I told him to go right on in. I didn't even think to ask him anything."

CHAPTER SEVENTEEN

 he Cable Creek Hotel was an old and run-down affair. Its better days were now long gone, and it stood alone on the highway as a reminder of better times. What used to be the go-to place for the small village was now a dump for the ne'er-do-wells and those down on their luck. When the squad car drove into the parking lot, O'Malley was sure that I had been mistaken, but because of my determination, he was equally determined to see it through.

The blinking vacancy light was dull and only flashed intermittently, and the foliage that should have beautified the place had all but withered up from lack of care. If it hadn't been for the frequent rains that fell on Ireland, it would have all died years ago.

I got out of the car and stood there, my eyes aghast at the sight.

"This is it?" I asked, incredulous.

"Yes, this is it."

"I can't believe that this place is still open for business."

"Trust me, this place doesn't do the kind of business that you want to dabble in."

I hunched up my shoulders. "Oh well, this is your area of expertise."

O'Malley cocked one eyebrow. "Serious? You're going to let me take point on this?"

I nodded and gave him a sheepish grin.

"All right, you just stay behind me."

"Will do, Captain." I laughed and gave a clumsy salute.

He rolled his eyes and mumbled, "Americans," under his breath.

"All right, let's go."

Two more squad cars had come in behind us.

"You two cover the other exits, and we'll go in the front," O'Malley directed them.

"He's in Room 218," O'Malley said then turned to me. "Remember, stay behind me."

"Gotcha."

I felt like I was in the movies. We climbed up the stairs slowly, O'Malley watching for the slightest movement. We paused a couple of times before we reached the door. It was exciting. I can't remember when my heart was racing so fast. One of the other officers approached the door from the other side, his gun drawn and ready in case there was trouble. They nodded to each other when they were ready, and O'Malley knocked loudly on the door.

"Police! Open up!"

There was a resounding crash from inside the room, and then silence.

"Police! Open up!" he shouted again, this time not as forceful.

Still there was no response from inside.

O'Malley took the room key he had gotten from the manager and unlocked the door.

"Police!" he called again as he pushed it open wide. They entered slowly, making sure that I stayed outside until I got the all clear. There was no one inside, but they found the window to the patio wide open. Had the perp jumped from the balcony to the floor below and ran off? I walked around the room, looking over every-thing. There were files of every property owner in Cable Creek and detailed information about each of them.

"Look at this," I said as I handed O'Malley a folder.

He thumbed through it. "Jeez," he said out loud. "This guy wanted to buy up every piece of property in town."

"He approached me at the coffee shop in town the other day. I didn't think anything of it, but I didn't like him very much. He wanted me to convince Mrs. O'Brian to sell to him."

"Well, sadly we didn't get a bead on him in time. It is unfortunate that the O'Brians had to suffer from his greed."

"The good news is that no one else will have to. And Mrs. O'Brian will be okay."

"Look here," he said, pointing to a name on his list of many. "It's your grandmother's property here, too."

I gasped at the sight of it.

"You should be happy. If it weren't for you, it may have taken us months to figure this guy out."

"But why was he staying here in this dump?" I wondered out loud.

"My guess was so he could fly under the radar. No one notices people in places like this. He couldn't have gotten away with so much if he had been in one of our upscale B&Bs. The people that stay there tend to draw attention."

I let out a long breath. "At least I'm glad it's all over and my grams is safe."

O'Malley's radio sprang to life.

"O'Malley here," he answered.

"Suspect has been apprehended."

"Did you say apprehended?"

"Yes, sir. We caught him trying to run into the woods."

"You're sure?"

"Sure, sir. I've got eyes on him right now."

The news was like music to my ears. Up until that point, I hadn't realized how tense I had been. The constant worry about Grams had pushed me through to the point of exhaustion, but as soon as I had heard that Colin had been captured, I could finally breathe a sigh of relief.

I couldn't wait to tell Grams that it was all over. I knew she would be relieved, too. But my heart still felt sad for Mrs. O'Brian and all that she had to go through. But, from what I could see, she was just as tough as my grams, and they would do well together.

I had O'Malley take me straight to the hospital to share the good news. Before he had brought the car to a complete stop, I was already trying to open the door to the car and sprint, but he had a lock on that could only be released when he decided. I gave him a critical look, and he simply laughed but only for a few seconds, then he released me and I was off in a flash.

I only slowed down when I reached Mrs. O'Brian's

room. She was still weak and recovering, and I didn't want to get her too excited.

"What happened?" she and my grams both asked as soon as I entered the door. I guess I hadn't calmed down enough.

"We got him!" I shouted, then put my hand over my mouth to force myself to be quieter.

"You got him?" Grams asked.

"Yes, they caught him trying to flee into the woods."

"Wonderful!" Grams clapped her hands together and leaned over Mrs. O'Brian to give her an excited hug.

I fell into a chair and tried to catch my breath.

"Oh, thank you so much," Mrs. O'Brian whispered to me. "You have done so much to help me. I don't know how to thank you."

"You just did," I said softly, reaching over and taking her hand in mine.

"Patrick would have loved you so much. You already feel like a daughter to me."

I cast a happy eye over to Grams, who only smiled back.

O'Malley came in a few minutes later. "I guess you've heard the news," he said quietly.

"Yes, we did!" Grams said excitedly and ran over to give him a hug. "Yes, we did. That was fine work you boys did, just fine."

"Well, I have to admit, we couldn't have done it so quickly without the determination of Annabelle. She really kept us on our toes."

"She's like that, you know."

He looked over at me. "Ever think of a job in law enforcement?"

"Don't think so," I told him. "My goals are much simpler than that. I'm thinking about something just a little bit more subdued than that. My life in New York is filled with bad guys. I want to work with some good guys for a change."

He smiled and walked over to Mrs. O'Brian. "I'm glad you're feeling better now. What did the doctor say?"

"He told me that I've turned the corner, and I should be going home soon." A cloud of sadness covered her face.

"Don't you worry, dear," Grams cooed. "You go home when you're ready, and I'll help you every step of the way."

"Me too," O'Malley said.

"I don't know about you guys, but I'm exhausted," I said. "I want to go back to Gladstone and sleep for a week."

"Me too," Grams chimed in.

We all said good-bye to Mrs. O'Brian and headed

outside. Grams was holding onto my arms tightly; I thought she would cut off my circulation.

"I'm so proud of you," she said softly. "You couldn't have made me any happier than you did these last few days."

"Same here, Grams. Same here."

"I'm curious," O'Malley interrupted as we continued walking. "How did you figure it out so fast?"

"I guess it's my New York instincts. I trust them."

"I still don't understand how all the pieces fit together."

"Well, my first clue was the excitement Mr. O'Brian caused that first night at dinner. He claimed he had bugs running across his feet, but with more than twenty people looking, no one saw not even one bug."

"So, you knew it was poison?"

"No, not then, but I felt it had something to do with it. It was when I found the medical alert bracelet in the bathroom. At first, I thought it was Lillian's, but when she told me it didn't belong to either of them, I had to figure out how it fit in. But before I could do that, I had to find out a motive."

"That was the hardest part," Grams said. "The O'Brians were liked by everyone."

"And that meant that it had to be someone from

outside the community. Cable Creek is a tight-knit group; no one here had any problems with them."

"I was beginning to wonder about that," O'Malley said. "Everyone we talked to had nothing but praise for them."

"Then I remembered when Colin Murphy approached me about talking to Mrs. O'Brian that I started to suspect the possibility that it could be him. He had a cough when I spoke to him at the coffee shop, but even then, it took me a while to put it together. All our focus was on the guests, none of us were thinking about the workers. They walk around like invisible people, and no one ever notices them."

"No one except Grams here," O'Malley said.

"That's when I put it all together."

"But I still don't get it. What were all those yellow flecks on the wall?"

"When I realized that it was Colin who had pretended to be a waiter, it kind of all fell into place. I had spent the whole night researching aconite toxicity. The toxin is sold in many herbal stores as a common treatment for anxiety disorders and is fine when taken in very small amounts. I figured he was smart enough not to purchase it in a small town like Cable Creek. If he did, everyone would have known it was him. We see how fast news travels in small towns like this. But he didn't have to buy it; aconite is found in the petals of many of the flowers around us. It would have been easy for him to get a few flowers, crush the petals, and add it to the lotions or creams or even the denture cream that the O'Brians used. All he needed was a few minutes in the bathroom to get the toxin in and he was all set." I paused and looked at O'Malley. "I would venture to guess that if you take a sample of those yellow flecks we saw in the bathroom, you'll find aconite."

"But Mr. O'Brian started having symptoms the night before."

"Yes. Colin posed as a waiter so he could secretly add a little to Mr. O'Brian's drink. Just enough to trigger a reaction. He might have just been testing it to see if it was potent enough. Or maybe he was trying to get a lesser reaction that would make everyone think he was losing his mental ability and bring his judgment into question."

"It is possible."

"He probably waited until Lillian left for breakfast to come in to finish the job. It would have taken only a few minutes to introduce the toxin and get out without being noticed. He may not have had enough time to clean up his work and had to leave by the sliding door to the balcony. That's why it was left slightly open." I paused a moment. "We know he paid

Mrs. O'Brian a visit when he realized that she was not going to sell the property either, and added a little poison to the flowers he brought. Unfortunately for him, Liam recognized him from the photo on his business card."

"And he went through all of this for what? To get his hands on that land?"

"Yes. He thought the O'Brians were getting in the way of his plans to build a new and modern development here in Cable Creek."

"He almost got away with it, too. So subtle."

"But what was the deal with the medical alert?" Grams asked.

"I can answer that," O'Malley interjected. "Once we learned that the alert bracelet did not belong to either of the O'Brians, it was easy to figure out. All of these emergency alerts are registered with a service that monitors their use. When something happens, they can alert paramedics right away. I took the alert back to the company listed on the back to find out who was registered to that device."

"And what did you find out?"

"It turns out it was an unregistered device."

I nodded. "Leaving it in the bathroom would also add to the illusion of Mr. O'Brian having a problem with his memory."

"Yeah. Probably wanted it to appear that he couldn't even remember to wear his own medical alert."

"Though, Mrs. O'Brian told me he never took his off," I put in. "Where was his actual device?"

"The ironic thing is, Mr. O'Brian forgot it at home before going to the castle. Maybe by accident, or maybe he didn't think he needed it, for whatever reason. I'm not sure if our perp wasn't aware if he had one or not, but it really seems like he wanted to cement a certain perception of a memory problem... He probably thought that if people started to believe that, then it was quite possible they would believe that he could fall ill and not be able to get the help he needed."

"It's so sad. He went through all of that just to get the O'Brians' land."

"It's a nice piece of land," Liam offered. "You really should go up to see it while you're here. Once you do, you'll understand why he went through so much trouble."

"Unfortunately, his plans to get rid of the O'Brians was just the beginning," Grams said sadly. "He had no idea that he was going to hit a wall with every landowner in town."

"I know it's a sad ending for Lillian, but it will serve as a lesson for anyone else who wants to try to get their hands on our property," Liam added.

"All thanks to Annabelle," O'Malley said. "Seriously, you need to think about a life in law enforcement."

I laughed a little. "Not me. I'm not strong enough for that."

We were in the parking lot now.

"Come on, Grams," I said, wrapping my arm around her waist. "Let's go home."

She smiled. "I'm for that."

We said good-bye to O'Malley and Liam and headed back to my favorite place in the world. Gladstone.

# # #

Thank you for reading! Want to help out?

Reviews are a crucial for independent authors like me, so if you enjoyed my book, **please consider leaving a review today**.

Thank you!

Penny Brooke

ABOUT THE AUTHOR

Penny Brooke has been reading mysteries as long as she can remember. When not penning her own stories, she enjoys spending time at the beach, sailing, volunteering, crocheting, and cozying up with a good book. She lives with her husband and their spunky miniature schnauzer, Lexi, and two rescued felines, George and Weezy.